Pinocchio's Sister

Jan Slepian

Pinocchio's Sister

PHILOMEL BOOKS NEW YORK

Book design by Sue H. Ng.
The type is set in Meridien.

Library of Congress Cataloging-in-Publication Data
Slepian, Jan.   Pinocchio's sister / Jan Slepian.   p.   cm.
Summary: Feeling humiliated after a family scandal, a
ventriloquist on the vaudeville circuit turns inward, neglecting his
ten-year-old daughter and lavishing attention on his puppet.
[1. Fathers and daughters—Fiction. 2. Family problems—
Fiction. 3. Ventriloquism—Fiction. 4. Vaudeville—fiction.
5. Performing arts—Fiction.] I. Title.
PZ7.S6318Pi   1995   [Fic]—dc20   94-13610   CIP   AC
ISBN 0-399-22811-X

10 9 8 7 6 5 4 3 2 1   First Impression

To my vaudeville family—
Uncle Frank, Aunt Myrtle, Iris, and Mike

PROLOGUE

Fee Faw Fum. I'm about to tell you a scary story.

Don't look behind you or under the bed. This isn't about monsters or ghosts. The scariest stories are real ones with real people in the grip of bad feelings. It is burning jealousy and bitterness and carelessness with love which are the monsters in this story. They will lead us to what happened. They will take us to the final horror.

To tell it we go back to an earlier time, a time when you could step up to the box office of your local theater and for a quarter or fifty cents you could see live acts on the stage. It was called vaudeville.

There were jugglers and trained animals and magicians and acrobats and comical dancers and lady singers and every other kind of act. There were nine acts in all, one after the other. You could stay all day and if you weren't caught you could stay to see the whole show over again at night.

Movies were young then and soon they would push this kind of variety show offstage and send it the way of the dinosaurs. But not yet.

Now, the year is 1928 and we are in a darkened theater. The orchestra strikes up. The curtain rises and footlights kindle the stage.

It's vaudeville time.

CHAPTER 1

The girl straddled her carpetbag and sat on it, waiting for her father to finish his inspection of the theater in front of them. They had just gotten off a hot dusty bus and were on their way to the boarding-house that would be their home for the next week.

It was late afternoon in the small resort town of Ashburn, Ohio. The sun was low, making long shadows on the sandy pavement. A worn suitcase rested at the feet of the man. In one hand he held a long narrow black case as if it contained the family fortune, which in a sense, it did.

Mr. Rosedale and his ten-year-old daughter were traveling vaudevillians. He was a ventriloquist, and Martha was part of his act.

She was not what you would call a pretty child. Her hair was long and chocolate-brown, worn in two braids down her back. Her face was too pale, too anxious for her years. But there was also a touching sweetness to her delicate features.

She watched her father closely, keeping her fingers crossed in her lap, hoping he would approve of the theater. It might put him in a good mood.

After a long moment, his examination done, Mr. Rosedale pushed back his straw hat and nodded to the dignified brick building in front of him. "It'll do," he grunted. Long experience enabled him to judge the size of the stage and the number of seats in the audience without putting a foot inside the theater. "Hope the dressing rooms are decent," he added. That, he could never tell in advance. Where to change clothes and get ready for the act was usually a backstage pain in the neck. Rehearsals began the following morning, and he would learn about his dressing room soon enough.

He mumbled this to the air, but the girl squatting at his side heard him. A smile crossed her solemn face, changing it. Her eyes crinkled and her lips lifted with amusement. She was remembering the dressing room they had just left in a theater in Cleveland. It was a tiny space under the hot-water pipes, and so hot in that room that her father's makeup had melted like candle wax. Over their heads they could hear every jump and thump of the actors. Also they had to share the room with Mr. Ted Kadota. He was billed as Blimpo the Human Garbage Pail and weighed a ton. She had to sit on the dressing table when he squeezed himself in the dressing room, but

4

he was kind and had given her a stick of gum. She had liked him.

Her father was done. The pair picked up their bags and walked on past the souvenir shops and convenience stores that lined the main street.

The town was bordered at one end by Pete's Texas Barbecue and at the other end by a bakery that had people dreaming of its glazed doughnuts all winter. It was the kind of resort town that came awake for the families on holiday for the few months of summer. Then, after Labor Day, when school started, it emptied out and went back to sleep. Now, in early July, it was in full swing. The sidewalk was gritty with sand from the shores of Lake Erie. The Great Lake spread out behind the town all the way to infinity.

As they walked along, the man and his daughter were jostled by families returning from the beach to get ready for supper. Sun-scorched children, mothers laden with pails and towels, fathers carrying beach chairs hurried along the sandy pavement. The sharp smell of drying wool from their long black bathing suits followed them like a low pungent cloud.

The Rosedales made an odd pair in this crowd, getting curious sidelong glances from the passersby.

Martha's father was wearing his checked traveling suit and stiff white collar. His neat black moustache

5

was waxed at the tips and curved upwards, giving him a theatrical, almost comical look. But there was nothing comical in his long face and embittered eyes. The moustache was not for effect or vanity. It was simply useful in hiding the slight movement of his lips when he did his act.

Martha had on her gray high-buttoned shoes and long-sleeved best for travel. She wasn't aware that her dress was too long for style, giving her a quaint old-fashioned air. Her long braids and outmoded dress made her seem not quite of this world.

Altogether, neither of them was wearing the casual, unbuttoned look so typical of a beach resort. But they were used to curious stares from the outside world. Actors on the stage were considered an odd, loose lot, not a bit like ordinary people.

Around the corner from the theater, Mr. Rosedale stopped and checked the address of the brown-shingled boardinghouse with the one on the piece of paper in his hand. They climbed the few steps to the wide wraparound porch and rang the doorbell.

An ample, rosy-faced woman greeted them at the door. Yes, she had a double room available.

He handed her a card and she read aloud, ''Iris and Mr. Rosedale.'' She looked up at him with a broad smile. ''Sure,'' she said. ''I know you! You're the ventriloquist. I saw you once. I caught your act some years back in Ashtabula.''

She pointed to the long case he carried so carefully. "Is that Iris in there? Your puppet? She's some cutie, I'll tell you. Maybe she wants a room of her own." She laughed in a good-natured way, but Mr. Rosedale did not join her. Neither did the girl at his side.

"How did you hear about me?" The landlady leaned against the doorframe, ready to chat. They might have been sitting in the parlor.

"News travels on the road. Clean sheets and good food at Mama Pelosi's is what I heard."

"You heard right. This your little girl?"

"My daughter, Martha. Martha, say hello to Mrs. Pelosi."

"Call me Mama, sweetheart, everybody does," said Rosie Pelosi. She smiled down at the girl, and her glance narrowed. There was something about the young girl that caught her attention. The pale face was too anxious for her years. Those big dark eyes held an appeal akin to hunger. She noticed buttons missing on the too-long dress.

To Mr. Rosedale she said, "No Mrs. Rosedale traveling with you?"

"No." He didn't enlarge on this, and his forbidding tone told the landlady to change the subject.

She shrugged off her curiosity and said, "Well, perhaps you remember my act? A singer by the name of Rose LaRose?" She asked this with a little flirtatious toss of her head that was meant to recall for him a youthful songstress.

He was sorry. He didn't know her act. There was no time when you're on the road.

"True, true, don't I know. Well, come on in. We have some other acts booked for the Odeon staying here. A whole week's run!" She shook her streaked blond head in wonder and admiration. "When I was on the road it was mostly a different town every day. When I think of trying to get my costume decent in them run-down hotels, most of the time without an iron . . ." She winked at Martha. "Makes me glad I turned landlady."

Mama Pelosi handed Mr. Rosedale a key. "Upstairs to the left, last door. Dinner bell in half an hour."

Martha heard a scratching noise from someplace nearby. To one side of the staircase was a large dining room with a round table already set. Beyond the dining room was a door, and it was from behind that door that she heard frantic scratching and a high whimper.

Mama Pelosi, who was ushering them to the stairs, yelled to the noise, "Be quiet, Sparkle Bob! I'm coming. Keep your shirt on!"

There was a dog in the house! Maybe Martha could hold him and pet him. An unexpected gift.

The scratching stopped and then started up again.

Mrs. Pelosi made an irritated sound and headed for it, apologizing and pointing the way upstairs.

Once in the room, the man laid the long black case carefully on one of the twin beds and sank down beside it. He looked about the room without interest. As he lost himself in thought, he sighed heavily, as if a weight sat on his chest. Gloom sat on him like an extra set of clothes.

His daughter stood at the foot of the bed watching him, but trying not to let him know it. She mustn't speak to him yet. There was a ritual to their arrival at a new place that she mustn't disturb.

Mr. Rosedale slowly raised his arms and from his neck removed a thin gold chain. On it was a small key. With it he opened the black case on the bed and removed a wooden puppet. He sat it on his lap.

It was a carved child, a pretty girl puppet about the same age as Martha. She had on a white ruffled dress made of fine eyelet cotton. It was shot through with narrow blue ribbons. Her tiny feet were encased in black, strapped shoes of gleaming patent leather. On her head was a mass of golden curls and on her red-painted lips a perpetual sassy smile. Her round cheeks bulged like little apples. Blue eyes stared blankly up at the ceiling.

Mr. Rosedale stretched out his long supple fingers and closed them again as if he were going to play the piano. Then he reached a hand inside the back of her

9

head. The levers he grasped moved the blond head from side to side. The jaw moved up and down, the eyes closed and opened. Instantly, in some mysterious way, the doll became alive. As he checked her works, she seemed to be a living, breathing child sitting on her father's lap.

As he held his puppet, he too came alive. Gone was the gloom. Instead of a sour silence, he became positively merry. It was as if the puppet on his lap gave him life instead of the other way around.

"Well, nice to see you again," the puppet said, rolling her eyes up to his. "I thought I'd never get out of that case. Where've you been?"

"Busy, Iris, busy. You know how it is. Take a look around. This is our room for a whole week. What do you think?"

"It's no palace, that's for sure. Well, what can you expect from these two-bit places?" She rolled her eyes at an imaginary audience, and in a most amusing way said, "Help, help!" It was more or less her signature and always got a laugh.

Martha turned away. She didn't want to watch. They were both too much together, shutting her out.

Instead, she walked around the room, touching everything. She always did this before she unpacked. It helped make the room more familiar, more like being in a place that she knew and that knew her.

Their twin beds had brass bedposts at both ends. They were side-by-side and covered by identical white bedspreads. Tiny white tassels were attached all over the spread. She smoothed them down so they all faced the same way.

Opposite the beds and against the wall was a square wooden stand covered by a white doily. On it sat a large blue bowl and a pitcher of water for washing up. The towels were a bit rough to Martha's touch, but clean.

Above the washstand was a mirror. In it she could see Iris on her father's lap. His face was bent to the puppet. The bright yellow hair and red lips and vivid cheeks seemed to draw all the color in the room. For a single moment she gazed at her own pale face and turned away quickly. But not before that familiar sickening twist in her belly.

Next to the washstand was a curved dresser. She ran her finger along the rim. The wood smelled lemony to her and felt like velvet.

Next to examine were two wooden straight-backed chairs. On one of them the cane seat was unraveling. She pulled at the stiff strand, but it wouldn't break off.

There was an oval rag rug in the middle of the room. She lifted a corner and saw that it covered a worn spot on the wooden floor.

All this time she knew Iris was watching her.

Those blue eyes were following her. As if the puppet knew about the pain that twisted her belly at rehearsal time and how she couldn't stand to watch any more. It occurred to Martha that she must be more careful about her thoughts around Iris.

She ran to the window and pulled up the beige paper shade so she could lean out. She leaned out further. Clumps of trees in the yard next door kept her from seeing the lake that she knew was there.

Disappointment had her bite her lips. She had dreamed of being able to see the big lake and to hear the waves from her bed.

She pulled her head back from the window, thinking to tell her father this. Maybe they could get a different room, a room where she could see the water.

One look at his face changed her mind. He had put Iris back in her case and was looking inward again, thinking of his troubles, of what he had lost. Bitterness was there, solid and severe enough to stop the words in her mouth.

A kind of homesickness washed over her. She wanted her father the way he used to be. The time before the trouble when Iris was just a puppet and Martha was the one who owned his lap.

She was ready for the secret part of her own ritual. She pulled two hairs from her own dark head. She twisted them together and released them to the air. As she did so, she said her wish: "Please let him like me better than her."

Now she was ready to unpack.

CHAPTER 2

🎭**M**artha unpacked her everyday clothes. She hung her stage dress in the narrow closet. It was a rag of a dress, gray as a rat and torn at the hem and sleeve. The dress was just for the act. She knew that. But still . . . She thought of what Iris wore, all ruffles and bows. The puppet's pretty white dress that her father washed and ironed so carefully. Someday she was going to change things around, and she'd be the one to wear the white ruffles. She'd put the ratty old dress on Iris and the pretty one on herself. Wouldn't her father be surprised.

The dinner bell sounded from someplace downstairs. Mr. Rosedale hadn't moved from the bed.

"Daddy? We have to go down. Don't you want to eat?" For the umpteenth time that day she examined his face. How sad he looked when he wasn't working. She couldn't help herself. She threw her thin arms around his neck. Her father didn't seem to notice. "Daddy, come on." Unsaid, but buried in those words were other ones: Daddy, don't forget me. Daddy, look at me. I'm here.

He roused and patted her absently. "Yes, yes. Just a minute. I have to wash up."

His face and hands dried, he bent at the knee to check himself in the small mirror above the washstand. He smoothed back his dark hair with the heels of his hands and twirled his moustache ends to make them stand up.

He attempted a smile at his daughter, but it was a hard time of the day for him. What was waiting for him downstairs was dinner-table talk. Nothing to look forward to. He picked up Iris's case and said, "Let's go." He always took Iris with him. Even the weight of the case in his hand made him feel stronger, safer, more like a man.

They weren't the first or last in the dining room. Two other men and a lady were already seated.

As they paused at the doorway, Martha noticed there were a lot of empty chairs at the big round table that almost filled the room. The maroon-fringed chandelier spread a friendly circle of light over the white tablecloth. A heavy oak sideboard held extra plates and silverware, baskets of bread, and a large salad bowl. The bold red stripes of the wallpaper were largely hidden behind rows of photographs of a younger Rosie Pelosi in her vaudeville days. These were publicity photos of Rose LaRose in full splendor of costume and makeup in various glamour poses. All in all it was a cozy room, and it smelled of good food.

This was always the hard part for Martha—to enter a new dining room and say hello to strangers who stared at her with curious eyes. She had always been a shy child, but since the scandal and her father's shame it was even harder for her to meet people who might know about it. There was always the chance one of them might start something. Bring up the subject. Someone might mention her stepmother. The suspense of what might be ahead made it hard to take the step inside.

As she and her father moved to the table, she glanced around swiftly under lowered lids to see if Mama Pelosi's dog was someplace in the room. Sprawled at the foot of the chair nearest the kitchen was an enormous white Labrador, resting his big head on his paws.

Martha left her father's side and dropped to her knees beside the dog. He was too big to hold in her arms, but she could pet him, smooth his fur, show him she was a friend. Martha had just been handed a piece of heaven.

Mr. Rosedale saw her reach out to the animal and he swooped to stop her. The dog might bite. Mama Pelosi at that moment came through the swinging door, carrying a large platter. She set it on the sideboard and laughed at what she saw. "Don't you worry about Sparkle Bob, Mr. Rosedale. He wouldn't hurt a fly. Unless of course a fly was trying to hurt me. You can pet him, Martha."

Martha wondered why he had been so unhappy earlier. "He was scratching at the door and whining something awful." Mama Pelosi made a humorous face at her dog. "Yeah, he suffers when I leave him. Worse than a jealous husband, he is."

At the sight of his mistress, Sparkle Bob lumbered to his feet and followed her around the table. The dog was so big his nose was even with the table. Martha couldn't take her eyes from him. She had never been so close to such a big dog before. Black eyes, black nose, white face, he looked like a seal, she decided. Or maybe a polar bear.

Sparkle Bob wasn't interested in the food, only in Rosie Pelosi. He followed her every movement as if to say, Oh boy, oh joy, she's here. The light of my life. My one and only. I'll never let her out of my sight again. Now and then the wagging of his tail caught in the tablecloth and lifted it, making it balloon out.

"Sit, sit" urged Mama Pelosi to the Rosedales. "Anyplace. You are about to have a treat. The famous one and only Rosie Pelosi meatballs. Ta Da! The secret is in the Mozzarella cheese and plenty of parsley."

She clucked her tongue at the sight of the empty chairs and went to the staircase. She called up, "Yoo-hoo, Pliskas. Come. Dinner. Don't let it get cold."

To the people at the table she explained, "Acrobats. Polish, I think. A big family. Nobody speaks English except the boy. It's a . . ." She broke off to give an order to her dog, who had followed her to the staircase and was tangling himself in her skirt. "Bob, go over there and sit down!" Then she completed her sentence. "It's a dumb act."

Martha knew enough vaudeville talk to understand that she didn't mean the Pliskas' act was stupid. Acrobats were called a dumb act because there was no talking in it.

Sparkle Bob padded back to the chair of his beloved at the head of the table. Before he sat, he looked at his mistress with a look in his eyes that said, How could you do this to me! How could you send me away when I love you so?

Martha stretched out a hand to him. He gave it a lick out of politeness. At this attention a spurt of joy rose and took hold of her.

Her father told her to sit down and grunted a hello to the man sitting next to him.

A bald man with a short, pointed beard grinned at him and nodded. "Long time no see, Rosedale. Tulsa, if I'm not mistaken. The Keith circuit. Two, three years ago. Yes. Wasn't there a blizzard? I seem to recall there were more people onstage than in the audience. Well, no question, we're losing out to these newfangled talking pictures. Soon we vaudes will be doing our acts on street corners. This your girl? I don't recall her."

"Yes. My daughter, Martha. She was in boarding school at the time. She's with me now. Part of the act. Martha, say hello to Mr. Ned Murphy, otherwise known as Kazzam, the Master of Magic."

Kazzam leaned across her father to pull a dinner roll from Martha's ear. He handed it to her. "Your roll, Miss Martha. That's a funny place to keep it. You keep butter there, too? Here, let me see." Martha giggled and pulled away. She didn't want any butter in her ear.

She looked about the table and inwardly smiled. This was a nice place. Maybe tonight will go well. The room seemed brighter because the man had made her laugh. Mama Pelosi was funny, and there was a great dog to play with. It didn't take much to send her spirits way up or way down.

The pretty lady across the way asked the others, "Say, who's the headliner? Anybody know? We just got in from Dayton. We're the Taylors, by the way. The Dancing Taylors? This is Norm, my partner. Husband also, worse luck." She lifted a thumb to the slender man next to her wearing a green striped suit and a boozy vacant smile. "I'm Noreen to my friends." She grinned at Martha, who was entranced by her dangling earrings and the spit curls that decorated the rouged cheeks.

There were exchanges of nods. None of the entertainers knew who the headliner was, but Rosie Pelosi did. "I hear you have Glenda Blue on the bill," she said. "I know the manager of the theater, Larry Beck. He told me."

"Hey, I've heard of her!" said Noreen Taylor with lively interest. "Isn't she the one that wiggles and shakes it across the stage? She's a wild one. I hear they take bets on whether her teeth will fall out."

Her partner, Norm, raised a hand to his tie and said, "Wow." He bugged out his eyes as if seeing something hair-raising.

Rosie said, "Yeah. Now I ask you, what does she have that I don't have? Just youth and fame and beauty, that's all. And, not to forget, a body that can shake like a bowl of jelly. But I ask you. Can she sing like this?"

Here Rosie struck a pose, opened her mouth, and belted out a few bars of some long-ago song, "A kiss from your lips will snap my suspenders," she sang, her voice loud and brassy and full of humor.

Martha clapped her hand over her mouth to muffle the shriek. Mama Pelosi was so funny.

After the applause and general laughter it was Norm, the dancer, who leaned forward and said the unsayable. "Say, Rosedale, I heard about the Mrs. Tough luck, leaving you flat like that. The man should be horsewhipped. I hear they run off without even a so-long. That so? Too bad for the act, eh?"

The table fell silent. His pretty wife flushed and spoke up quickly. "Don't mind Norman, Mr. Rosedale. Hoofers are awful gossips. It's none of our business. He's had a few too many. Haven't you?" she asked her partner. He opened his mouth to answer and she said, "Shut up."

This was the conversation that father and daughter had dreaded. The vaudeville circuit was like a private club, and everyone knew everyone else's business. The news of Martha's stepmother running off with George Roper, the comic juggler, was common knowledge. Roper was a headliner, a well-known entertainer. The details of the desertion went the rounds of the vaudevillians faster than flu. No matter what town the Rosedales landed in, someone was bound to bring it up. It had happened six months ago, but to the man she had abandoned and humiliated, it was still raw and recent. He always suspected that he was being laughed at behind his back.

Martha stared down at her plate. She had hardly known her stepmother and certainly didn't mourn her absence. But any talk of the runaways made her father worse. More inward, more stiff and standoffish.

Rosedale's hand moved absently in the air as if Iris were on his lap. If she were, he would have been able to spit out his bitterness at the world through her. It was as if the blood in his veins had turned to vinegar, biting and sour. To be a man alone, with a child to feed, one wife long dead, the other leaving him for riffraff. Where was justice in this world?

He made a move to take Iris out of the case at his feet, but changed his mind. Instead he glared at the offending man across the table. Suddenly, from the platter on the sideboard, one of the meatballs spoke up. "If that man opens his stupid mouth once more, I'm going to stuff myself down his throat." Mr. Rosedale's lips hadn't seemed to move at all.

"Hey, now!" Offended, Norm Taylor struggled to get to his feet. He was held back by his partner.

Mama Pelosi jumped into this awkward moment. She began to fill plates with food. As she ladled the first spoonful she said to the meatballs, "Not another word out of you. Hear me?" She clucked her tongue and said, "Fresh things." She grinned at Mr. Rosedale, who missed it. His head was down. He was still glowering.

This bit of amusement melted the frozen silence at the table. She passed the plates around and continued, "But wait till you taste my meatballs!

22

Manny, my late husband, was a terrific piano player, dear man, may he rest in peace. He loved my meatballs better even than my singing. I'll tell you something. We toured together in two-a-days all over this country for more years than I want to tell. He at the piano, me in a long dress with sparkles and singing those songs." She smiled with sad eyes at the pictures on the wall.

With a short laugh at herself, she said, "Say, my Manny could play anything at all if he heard it just once. He rode those keys like nobody's business. But believe it or not, the man couldn't read a note of music. How about that, Martha, my girl? Here, eat up, little one. It's not a funeral. A girl your age should smile a little. One bite and those creases in your forehead will disappear. I guarantee."

Her easy good nature made the child relax a bit. Something tight inside her loosened, allowing her to breathe. When her father and that awful man had their exchange, that something got tighter. It was as if a wire spring were winding itself up—someplace near her breathing, near her heart.

Outside the dining room there was a tumble of footsteps down the stairs. A dog yapped, a delicate high-pitched bark that made Sparkle Bob's ears perk up.

Mama Pelosi said, "Ah, at last. Here come the Pliskas."

CHAPTER 3

The clatter of rapid footsteps on the stairs, the staccato of a foreign language, and then a tumble of people crowded into the dining room all at once. The Pliskas were vivid as birds, three men, three women, and a boy. They were a troupe of Polish acrobats, new to the country, and booked for the week at the Odeon.

They stood in the doorway, sending shy smiles around the table. The women all wore white blouses heavily embroidered with jewel colors. Their skirts were long and Gypsy-like and on their heads were bright kerchiefs. The three men and the young boy had on white shirts and decorated vests worn over baggy black trousers.

Martha had seen a lot of costumes in her vaudeville life, but onstage not off. She gaped at them with big admiring eyes and thought they all looked gorgeous.

A small snout poked through the long skirt of the

24

older woman. A bright-eyed black poodle not much larger than a loaf of bread emerged from under the skirt and sat with head high in front of the woman as if waiting for applause.

Mama Pelosi put a restraining hand on Sparkle Bob to prevent him from investigating the tiny newcomer. He could have swallowed the dog in one gulp.

The short wiry boy with hair the color of straw went up to Rosie Pelosi. His English was accented and peculiar.

"Madam," he said and bent over her hand to kiss it in the European way. "My family says big regrets for lateness. We heard bell but do not know what means bell. So happy to know means dinner. Please forgive. Will not happen more."

Mrs. Pelosi rose, flustered at the hand-kissing, and tickled with the boy. She said, "Sure, kid. What's your name again?"

"Stanislaus Pliska. Call me Stashu." He had the manners and poise of a grown-up, but was no more than twelve years old. His grown-up airs dropped away when he saw Sparkle Bob. Then he was a boy like any other, on his knees, admiring and petting the huge dog.

The oldest man of the troupe said something sharp in his own tongue that made Stashu jump to his feet. He was being reprimanded for lack of manners. The boy hurriedly made introductions. His mother and father, Uncle Petra and Aunt Rima, brother Ladislaw and wife Jaslo. "All say to you a big hello and glad to be in America." Nods and smiles passed around the table.

Mama Pelosi urged them all to sit and pass their plates.

Meanwhile, the little trained poodle sat without moving in the doorway. Stashu called to her, "Lulu!" and held out his arms. The tiny creature rose to her feet, took a few steps, and leaped straight into his arms like a ballet dancer.

The boy held on to Lulu just in case Sparkle Bob turned nasty. The two dogs gave one another a thorough all-over acquaintance sniff. Stashu needn't have worried about an attack. On the contrary, it was love at first sight for Sparkle Bob. Mama Pelosi was number one on his human list, but Lulu instantly became top heartthrob in dogdom. The big Lab's tail went Wow! and his nose nudged her as if to say, One look is all I want. One look. Please. Is that too much to ask?

Lulu wasn't interested. She had turned her face up to Stashu, licking his face. Her heart was elsewhere.

The boy sat down and gave Lulu an order that had her sit unmoving at his feet. He was across the table from Martha and carefully avoided looking at her.

Martha stared at him. It was so seldom that she

was with another person so near her own age. There was that time at the boarding school, but she was too lonesome and miserable then for friends. But now there were two dogs in the house to love and another someone whom she could get to know and who might like her. He had looked so friendly when he came into the dining room. But now he didn't seem to know Martha was there, he hadn't even glanced at her.

She forced herself to make the first move. She gathered up her courage and said, ''Excuse me,'' to get his attention.

Stashu raised reluctant eyes to hers. He had been so easy with the adults at the table, but with Martha, a girl, and young like himself, his tongue wouldn't work.

''Can I pet your dog?'' she asked him. It was the first thing that popped into her mind.

He lowered his eyes and flushed. He didn't answer.

That did it. Martha wanted to disappear with embarrassment. He must hate her. She slipped to the floor beside Sparkle Bob, where she remained for the rest of the meal, passing a loving hand over his fur, scratching behind his ears, finding comfort where she could.

Finally her father was done. He picked up Iris, told Martha to say goodnight, and she was able to leave

27

the dining room, out of sight and sound of the boy who didn't want to speak to her. Every time she closed her eyes that night the scene replayed in her head. She heartily wished he would disappear by morning like Mr. Kazzam's magic dinner rolls and that she need never clap eyes on him again.

Backstage, at rehearsal the next morning, there he was. Stashu was at the back of the stage, turning handsprings in place, flipping over and over. Quickly Martha drew into the shadows so she wouldn't be seen. As she watched him at his practice, his skill amazed her.

He came to a full stop in a headstand. Lulu, his little poodle, sat beside him with her curly head cocked to one side, watching him like an anxious parent. Stashu bent his knees to his chin with his feet flat as a shelf toward the ceiling. On an order from him his dog leaped up to the soles of his feet. Stashu raised his legs in the air with the little dog sitting on his feet, as still and as balanced as an ornament on the hood of a car.

Upside down, the boy noticed Martha nearby, saw that she was watching him. She turned away before she saw his pleading smile.

She was careful not to trip over the ropes. The stagehands were busy, fixing spotlights, putting up the backdrops, shouting orders at one another. Everyone was getting ready for the afternoon matinee. Martha pressed herself against the heavy curtain, watching a different show from the one the paying audience would see.

The performers passed back and forth on the deep busy stage, some already in costume, some still in street clothes. They were preparing for their first rehearsal on a new stage with the orchestra. There was a lot of mumbling to the air, waving of hands, singing, juggling, tumbling. To an outsider it might seem like a time of utter confusion. But Martha understood very well that the entertainers were busy practicing their art, getting their act ready for a paying and critical audience.

The musicians were filing into the orchestra pit, some already seated and tuning their instruments. The orchestra leader was onstage in his shirtsleeves and suspenders, talking to the dance team from Mama's boardinghouse. All three were bent over some sheet music.

Martha drew in a deep breath. She smelled the backstage odors of greasepaint and dust and old ropes, of painted drop cloths and heated light, of sweat and strain and plain old stagefright. These were the smells of home to her.

She wandered to the wings of the stage and looked out at the empty seats of the music hall. The houselights were on, and in their hard glare she could now see something else that was usually secret from outsiders.

It was the theater without the make-believe. In the harsh light the velvet drapes were dusty along the walls, and faded in spots. Some of the gilt was chipped away from the beam across the balcony. The plush was torn on some of the seats, and the painted ceiling could use a touch-up.

Yet she knew that for the show that afternoon it all would be transformed. All it needed was living, breathing people taking their seats, the dimming of lights, the tuning up of the orchestra, the spotlight on the stage. Then, as if Cinderella's fairy godmother had waved a wand, the dusty drapes would disappear and the gilt would become real gold and the velvets glow like rubies. The actors would leave their everyday selves behind and would become whomever or whatever they wanted. Magic time would begin.

Onstage was Norm Taylor, the man who caused the trouble with her father the night before. He was still in his striped suit, showing stagehands where to set down a small round table and two chairs. His wife, Noreen, was already in full costume, a filmy full-skirted ball dress of lavender and cream. She placed a candle on the table and said, "Ready."

Martha hoped that he would be a flop and booed off the stage. At the same time she devoutly hoped his wife, Noreen, would be a big success. She had no idea how to have both wishes come true.

The two dancers sat and held hands across the table. The music struck up. They were acting out the story of a pair of aristocrats dining in some fancy restaurant. He stood before the beautiful lady, smoothed down his abundant hair, and invited her to join him on the dance floor. She was reluctant. He insisted.

She wafted to her feet and twirled into his arms. They floated off together, doing their steps, the perfect ballroom couple.

She missed a twirl and fell flat on the floor.

Martha's neck prickled with embarrassment. Oh, no, poor Mrs. Taylor. She certainly needed practice.

Mr. Taylor stopped the music to lean over the pit. He said to the orchestra leader, "Say, professor, could you give us a loud drumroll whenever we mess up. If you please."

So it was on purpose! Martha realized that the couple were a comedy dance team and that falling was part of the act.

The music started again and the Taylors resumed their dance. They were a skilled pair and danced beautifully until he put his head close to hers and came away spitting out hair. Boom! went the drum.

He made to kiss her hand and found himself kissing his own. Boom!

Again they were in perfect step until on a lift her evening dress fell over his eyes. He could no longer see where he was going. Holding her high above him, he staggered about the stage, nearly falling into the orchestra pit. A long drumroll.

Behind Martha someone said, "Would you like please to hold Lulu?" And there was Stashu, holding out the small dog to her like a present. His cheeks were flushed with shyness.

Martha's first impulse was to run away from him. She made as if to go, but Stashu held her arm and said, "Please." He held out his dog Lulu like a peace offering, and Martha couldn't resist her. The little dog went right to her, cuddled in her arms, and stayed there as quietly as a stuffed toy.

"Marta, I have to say you something," said Stashu.

"Martha. My name is Martha."

"Yes, Marta. What I want to say you is I am sincere with sorry. Last night you ask for to do something with Lulu and I don't know what is. I couldn't find word in my head. You understand me? I could say nothing. Please excuse and forgive."

"I asked to pet Lulu. Like this, see?" Martha ran her hand down Lulu's body in a long caress.

"Ah. Pet. I will remember. Marta, you will be friend with me? I never have American friend. Okay?"

Her big eyes examined him to see if he was teasing her. If so, she was ready to bolt. She looked closer. Maybe she had been wrong about him. He had a square open face, snub nose, and eyes the color of cloudless sky. She saw nothing bad there. She was about to blurt, I thought you hated me, but something about his hopeful face made her change it to, "Can I play with Lulu every day?"

"Ah, means friend? Good news! Yes to Lulu, but not now. Sorry. Now my family is for rehearse. Very needful of Lulu. You watch please?"

The Pliskas raced from the wings onto the stage one by one, all of them in spangles for their act. They flipped themselves into the air and turned head over heels as easily as tennis balls. They stood opposite one another in rows of three as Stashu was hurled and whirled in the air from one to the other like a spinning top. Sometimes it was Stashu, sometimes it was little Lulu who was tossed through the air. The orchestra followed each display of agility with a crash of cymbals or drumroll.

For the finale a small seesaw and high platform were wheeled out. Stashu stood at one end of the seesaw and his father climbed high up to the platform. The rest of the family formed a human ladder, one by one climbing upon each other's shoulders. Uncle Petra was the strongman on the bottom.

The father nodded to the orchestra leader and a

low drumroll began. Hardened and experienced actors hushed and stood about to watch the act. There was tension even among the performers who had seen everything before. They knew the dangers of a misstep, the necessity of absolute timing.

Stashu and his father exchanged a silent signal and Mr. Pliska jumped from his platform down to the upward end of the seesaw. This catapulted Stashu high into the air. One, two, three somersaults and he landed upright on the shoulders of the highest brother.

There was a spatter of applause from the wings, a rare tribute from other performers. But the act wasn't over yet. Stashu cried, "Lulu!" The little dog trotted to the seesaw and sat on the bottom end. Mr. Pliska jumped from his platform. Lulu was tossed high, high into the air, and by some miracle was caught by Stashu. He placed her on his head, where she sat up on her hind legs.

Martha knew a smash finish when she saw one. She began to clap and at that moment she felt a hand on her shoulder. One of the stagehands said to her, "Your father wants you, kiddo. Upstairs dressing room three."

She had remained backstage while her father was in the dressing room preparing Iris for the show. She didn't like to watch that part anymore. It hurt too much.

CHAPTER 4

Behind the stage was a spiral metal staircase that led to a row of upstairs dressing rooms. As she climbed, Martha clicked the tips of her shoes against the iron steps the way she used to when she wore taps on her shoes. She felt in the mood to dance. Stashu wanted to be friends. He didn't hate her. She had never had an acrobat boy for a friend before. Especially one who spoke such funny English.

The way her shoes tapped the iron steps reminded her of Tappy Hoyt, the dance man who had put taps on her shoes and taught her how to do a soft-shoe. Happy times, happy thought. How she had begged for those taps. She was maybe eight years old. It was back when her father did a solo act with Iris, when Martha was her father's girl and Iris was just his puppet.

Tappy was a friend, too. His real name was Henry and he told her he was saving up to go back home and buy a little grocery store with his brother. He used to travel with his own staircase, six steps in all. It was part of his act. Martha remembered how she used to watch his shiny patent-leather shoes dance up and down the steps, tapping out a rhythm that had everybody jumping.

Now Martha jumped her way to dressing room number three and stopped dancing. What was inside was nothing she wanted to see. She took a deep breath and opened the door.

Iris was on her father's lap. One of his hands was hidden in her curls, deep inside the puppet's head, where the levers made her move and look real. The other fussed with her dress, smoothed her blond hair.

"About time she decided to show up," said Iris, rolling her eyes at Martha. "Let's all skip rehearsal, why don't we?"

"Now, now, Iris, she's here now," rebuked Mr. Rosedale. "That's all that matters."

A father with his pretty, clever, impudent daughter. That was the illusion he set up and that was what the audience was supposed to see.

Martha saw what an audience saw. She knew better in her head. She knew it was just her father's wooden puppet on his lap. But in her heart, her soul, someplace where reason didn't reach, she saw her father fussing with his daughter Iris.

All the lightheartedness of minutes ago disappeared. What she wanted to do was to tear the wooden doll from his lap. Tear it away and toss it away. She wanted to yell at that painted face, "He's my father, not yours!"

Martha lowered her eyes to blot out the sight. Her blood was pounding in her ears with the force of her anger.

A voice deep inside her cried out, "Mother," but it was to no one she had ever known, and there was little comfort in the empty word. Her mother had died when Martha was born, and all there was left of her were pictures on a playbill and a few stories her father used to tell. She knew that her mother and her father had started the act together. Her mother was a singer, and the star of the act. Her father once told her that it was her mother who had trained his voice. She was the one who thought of using his singing in the act. Martha sometimes pored over the playbill pictures to see if she could find any resemblance to herself. But the young woman wrapped in furs with marcelled hair and dazzling smile and flirty dark eyes had nothing to do with Martha. She was too glamorous, too unreal to be anyone's mother, much less her own.

When her mother died, her father had continued the act as a solo, bringing up his baby girl on trains and in rooming houses. Trains and buses, one town after another, one boardinghouse or hotel room after another, no place was more home than another. That was a vaudevillian's life and the only one Martha knew. Her playground was the back of the stage. Her teachers were show people. The vaudeville acts were her schooling. Her father was her family, and Martha never wanted more or other than what she had.

She didn't miss a mother back then. There were always people in every show who petted and fussed over her. They begged for the chance to take care of her, many without children of their own, or whose children were away in school or with grandparents someplace. But it was her father who held her and took her temperature when she was sick, and read to her and listened to her dreams and allowed her to stay up and watch him from the wings. At the end of the act, just before his bow, he would turn his head and wink at her, a private signal, as good as a hug. She always waited for it.

And then it had all stopped.

It was that lady, the singer named Lily with the long legs and baby voice who had traveled the circuit with them two years ago. First she was just a replacement, a singer to take her mother's place in the act. Then her father fell crazy in love. He thought she was the most wonderful, most beautiful thing in the world. He had married her.

Martha was banished to a despised boarding school on Long Island. "For your own good," she

38

was told, but Martha knew that her stepmother didn't want her around.

When Lily ran off with the juggler, and her father came to take her from the school, Martha thought she would burst with joy. They would be together again.

But how changed it all was.

She glanced under her lowered lids at her father. He said, "Come. We rehearse."

The rehearsal had gone well. They had made themselves ready for the act.

Now the orchestra was tuning up, the matinee was about to start. It was time for her to sit in the audience and wait for her cue. The Rosedales were the second on the bill, a favored spot.

Martha was dressed in her rags, her eyes darkened to make her look sickly, her face powdered a stark white. She took the usual aisle seat in the back of the theater and watched the audience file in. The heavy curtain was closed, the stage was lit and ready. The families were hushing noisy children, and a giddy feeling of expectancy was in the air. Everyone was ready to be entertained.

The orchestra struck up. On either side of the stage was an easel with a large placard sitting on it. In fancy printing it told the audience the name of the act they were about to see: THE DANCING TAYLORS.

After their act was over, a stagehand replaced their placard with one that said, IRIS AND MR. ROSEDALE.

Martha's stomach knotted as it usually did before every performance.

The curtain parted. Her father sat on a chair in the middle of the stage with Iris on his lap. He was smiling, interested, good-humored, a straightman and fond father of the fresh kid on his knee.

Iris turned her head from one side of the audience to the other, looking them over. She said, "What time do they feed the animals around here?"

Her voice was high and teasing, full of laughter and sass. The audience roared and so did Iris.

"Now, now," said Mr. Rosedale gently, ever so slightly rebuking, smoothing things over. "Nice girls don't talk that way. Try to remember your manners."

She rolled her big blue eyes at the audience and said in a humorous, flippant way, "Help, help." People who had seen the act before said it with her. It got a laugh every time.

Her father said to Iris, "How about a song for these nice people?"

"Not on the stingy allowance you give me!"

That was Martha's cue. She rose from her seat in the back of the theater and ran down the aisle crying, "Papa, Papa, come home! Mama needs you. The baby is sick and we have no food!"

She was passed from one orchestra member to another and raised to the stage.

The audience saw a little girl in rags. Her plain little face was so pale, her eyes sunken. She must be starving, poor thing. The child fell to her knees and cried so piteously for her father to come home that there was a flurry of handkerchiefs in the audience. Eyes were mopped. Some of the more soft-hearted cried aloud, "Go, go on home!"

Mr. Rosedale said to Martha, "I'll come home with you, but first how about a song for the audience? Iris is a bad girl and won't sing for us. How about you?"

Martha stepped to the front of the stage, the orchestra struck up, and she sang a song her father had composed for her when she joined the act.

She sang:

Oh father, dear father, come home with me now
The baby is hungry and we sold the cow.

It was a song of struggle and strife that went well with her rags. She had a true, pretty voice and the audience gave her a big hand.

Iris said, "You call that singing? I could sing better than that when I was a toothpick! I'll show you."

"No, no, too late. You had your chance," said Mr. Rosedale. "No one is interested in hearing you sing."

41

Iris winked at the audience and said, "Oh, yeah? Why don't you ask them? What do you say, out there? Want to hear me sing?"

The audience whooped and clapped its approval and voices called out, "Go ahead!" "Let's hear it!"

Iris rolled her eyes at them and said, "Help, help."

When the laughter died down, Iris sang an aching love song.

What came from her was a shockingly beautiful voice, clear as a flute. The high pure sound rolled over the audience and hushed them. Children stopped wiggling in their seats as their mothers held them close. Men tightened their lips and nodded their heads at beauty. The song went straight to everyone's heart. When it was done it brought them to their feet.

Iris bowed right and left to the storm of applause. She seemed to be about to jump out of his lap. "Thank you, thank you," she cried. "Thank you, music lovers, one and all."

The audience ate her up. She made them laugh and she made them cry. She was pretty and she was bold. By the end of the act everyone in the theater forgot that Iris was just a puppet and applauded her as they would a real person.

Mr. Rosedale winked at Iris as she bowed.

Martha looked on, a smile pasted on her face.

If anyone had noticed the pale girl in whiteface

and rags, they would have seen something chilling in those dark eyes that didn't belong to a child.

Martha looked at Iris, and a thick, hot, sick pressure filled her chest. Jealous, jealous, her father had his hands on her. Iris filled her father's gaze. The puppet had the roar and applause of the audience; she was the focus of every eye. The doll was funny and clever and pretty and Martha was not.

Yes, she hated her. She hated what she envied. The spring wound tighter. A passion seized her. She knew now what she wanted.

CHAPTER 5

🐦 **T**he act ended with Martha pulling her father off the stage as if in a great hurry to get him "home."

Mr. Rosedale went immediately to his dressing room to take off his makeup and change from his tuxedo to his regular clothes. Martha, frightened by her own thoughts onstage, sought a private place to lean her head. She needed to catch her breath, or at least to catch up to her brain, which seemed to have something in mind that scared her.

There was a trick cyclist onstage now, and all was quiet behind his backdrop so as not to interfere with his monologue. Muffled laughter rose from the audience. The man who worked the curtain was dozing by his stool. A few performers waiting to go on chatted in whispers with one another. Some of the stagehands were taking advantage of a lull to play cards. Above them hung a naked lightbulb. Against the back wall, Larry Beck, the manager, was in deep conversation with a small frizzy-haired woman wearing a dress that looked like a shining sheath of silver. Martha realized this must be the headliner, Glenda Blue. Ordinarily she would have been fascinated and would have hung about to stare. Now all she wanted to do was to get away from the backstage cigarette smoke, the clots of whispering performers, the shadows, and her own thoughts.

Martha headed for a door behind the stage that led to the back alley. She needed the air, needed to go outside and see the sun. She would sit on the trash can and watch clouds like a normal person. In her dash, she tripped over some ropes and was caught before she fell by Stashu Pliska.

A smile spread across his good-natured face. "Oh, Marta, hello!" he said. "I am happy I see you. I hear you sing. Is very pretty. Also Iris, like girl Pinocchio. Your father, he very good, how you say? Make words come from other mouth?"

"My father's a ventriloquist. I'm sorry. I can't talk now, Stashu. I have to get out of here."

"Out from theater? But show not over." He peered at her closely. He saw her eyes. "What is matter, Marta? I see you trouble."

One hint of sympathy and that did it for Martha. What was pent up came out in a sob. She was glad she was still in costume and chalky makeup. She had the feeling that what was churning in her mind, spreading like a stain, would be written all over her face.

Stashu drew her to the back wall of the stage, where they could sit in shadow. They sat on the dirty floor and leaned against a ladder. He was in his spangled body suit, green and silver from top to bottom. It had no pockets for a handkerchief. He picked up the hem of her ratty dress and handed it to her to blow her nose.

After the first deep sob she had control of herself. She was not a crier. Her feelings were too deep and too scary for tears. There was no way to tell Stashu what was on her mind.

"Thanks," she said. "Don't mind me. I'm crazy."

"Not to worry. I like crazy," said the boy. He strummed his fingers on his lips like an idiot and crossed his eyes. He jumped to his feet and staggered about until he saw that he had won a faint smile from the troubled girl. Then he squatted in front of her and said, "Something bother you, I help. Just to ask."

He began to say something more, hesitated, and then let loose a string of Polish words that Martha knew were curses in any language. She was startled and got to her feet, ready to leave.

Stashu grinned at her. "Lucky for you, not know to speak Polish." She couldn't see his face too well in the dingy light, but she felt the force of his good nature and friendliness.

He said, "I angry at me, Stashu, not you. Grrrrr," he growled like a dog. "I speak English I sound like baby. Yes? I sound like stupid boy. Yes? I not say what is in here and here." He thumped himself in the head and heart. "In my language I am smart boy. Everybody say. In America I have no head. No tongue." He pulled at the offending organ in his mouth and pretended to cut it off with imaginary scissors.

"No, no, Stashu, stop that." She grabbed his arm, half laughing. He really was the funniest boy. "I know what you mean, honest I do. And thanks a lot. I mean it. I'm okay, really." She saw that he wasn't convinced. Martha looked at him straight and knew she could trust him. They hardly knew one another, but sometimes you can get a sense about a person right away. You can tell. She said in his ear, "If I need you. If you can help. I promise I will ask you."

She ran upstairs to the dressing room. Instead of dancing her way up, she took the metal circular steps two at a time. Her heart was thumping as loud as the drum in the orchestra, or so she thought. She hadn't told him anything. But now she had someone she could call on to help her if she needed him. That made what she was thinking more real.

Mr. Rosedale was at his dressing table, removing

47

the stage makeup that gave his ashen face its touch of health. He glanced briefly at his daughter when she burst in, and went back to creaming his face.

"Not bad, don't you think? It went well for the first show. You could have given your lines a little more feeling out there," he said to her. "And I want to change where you sing your song for tonight. You're too much front stage. I think you block Iris too much. What do you think, Iris?"

The puppet in her ruffles was propped up on the only other chair in the room. Her blond curls rested against the cushion and her jointed legs in their patent leather shoes were ruler-straight in front of her. The red cheeks bulged with laughter, and from the wide painted lips came, "How do you block a blockhead?"

Mr. Rosedale chuckled. "That's good, Iris. 'Block a blockhead.' Maybe I can use it in the act."

"Help, help," said the puppet, funny as always.

Martha stared at Iris in horror. She was certain that the impertinent blue eyes had rolled by themselves from one side to the other as the wooden mouth said, "Help, help."

Martha realized that she had to be extra careful from now on. Oh yes, she had to be clever and hide her thoughts in front of Iris. The puppet mustn't know what was on Martha's mind. She mustn't know what was going to happen to her.

48

She placed herself behind her father with her back to the puppet and said to his image in the mirror, "Okay, Daddy. Are we going to stay and rehearse now? Should I keep my costume on?"

They usually were free between the afternoon and evening shows. Most often it was the time when they could tend to their clothes or do a little shopping. But sometimes, in the long-ago days when her father was happy, they would go to a park together, or a playground, or have a picnic.

"No, we'll get back here and rehearse before the evening show. Right now I want to go back to the room. I'm tired to my very bones. And you, my girl, have to nap before tonight or else Mama Pelosi won't let me hear the end of it. She seems to think you're not well, which I told her was ridiculous. But she also says I neglect you."

He stopped creaming his face, his hand in midair, and looked at his daughter in the mirror. His melancholy eyes searched her face. "Do I neglect you, child?" he asked.

For a moment there was a real question in the air. He was truly seeing his daughter. He really wanted to know.

The feeling of being close to him again was overpowering to the girl. It was food and drink, all the nourishment she needed. Unable to answer such a question, she could only say, "Oh, Daddy," and lean her forehead against the back of his neck with her eyes closed. She breathed in the familiar combination of greasepaint and face cream. Her torment over Iris fled from her mind. She was filled with comfort. Her eyelids drooped and she was suddenly so tired. She would like to nap just where she was.

"Yes, well, these vaudevillians make a big drama out of everything," her father said. "I told her to mind her own business." The moment was over.

He handed her the jar of face cream. She removed her stage makeup and changed into her everyday cotton dress. She hung the ratty stage dress on the hook behind the door and said, "Okay, Daddy, I'm ready. Can we go now?"

Mr. Rosedale picked up Iris to put her in her case. He would be taking her back to the boardinghouse even though they were returning for the evening show. Never would he leave his puppet in the dressing room.

From around his neck he removed the gold chain that was usually out of sight, under his shirt. The tiny key dangled from it like a pendant. He lifted Iris from the chair and tucked her carefully into the black snakeskin carrying case. He closed the lid, locked it, and slipped the chain and key around his neck once again.

As Martha watched her father do that familiar routine, she imagined herself in the middle of the night, waking up, making sure her father was fast asleep, and then tiptoing over to where Iris slept out of sight, under the lid. She saw herself reaching out a hand and putting the key in the lock and turning it, and then . . .

The key! She had to have the key for what she wanted to do, had to do, needed to do. It was the only possible way. But her father was never without it. He never took it off, never, not even when he slept.

Now she realized she would have to get Stashu to help her. He was smart. He would have some ideas. She could never do what needed to be done by herself.

CHAPTER 6

🐾 **E**arly the next morning, when the sun had barely time to warm the sand, Martha and Stashu were up and out, walking the dogs along the beach.

At the dinner table the night before, Martha had managed to whisper to Stashu that she had to talk to him. In private. After a moment's thought he told her that he walked Lulu every morning, they could talk then. Martha had begged Rosie Pelosi to let her take Sparkle Bob, and it was all arranged.

A few sunbathers had their chairs out, and some hardy souls were already in the water. But the stretch of coarse sand between the cliff and surf was largely deserted except for a couple of early-morning fishermen casting from the jetty. The water looked cold, heaving gently in smooth tilting sheets. The surf was quiet as it lifted and left its lacy foam in arcs on the shore bank. Sandpipers raced after the receding water on their stick legs, pecking at invisible fruits of the sea. Gulls circled and swooped, filling the air with their wild lonesome cry.

Lulu picked her ladylike way along the shore without a leash, since Stashu had only to say her name or whistle a few notes and she was at his side. Her black nose was in the air, haughty as royalty, sniffing the fine day.

Sparkle Bob bounded along beside her in dogs' heaven. He alternately strained ahead at his leash in a burst of joyous spirits, or stopped short to explore an alluring smell. Every once in a while he returned to Lulu, crouched before her and sent a few hopeful barks her way, as if to say, "Hey, isn't this a great place! Want to play? Want to run? Want to watch me drag this kid in the sand?"

Martha held on to his leash tightly, but Sparkle Bob was a handful. Conversation wasn't easy when she was pulled across the sand every few minutes.

She and Stashu came across an old dried log that faced the water. She tied Sparkle Bob's leash to it so that they could talk in peace. The dogs settled down on their paws side-by-side like an old married couple.

Martha didn't know how to begin to tell Stashu what she wanted from him. She kicked the sand with her bare toes and pointed at the gulls and asked if he knew how to swim.

He brushed all that aside and straddled the log so he could face her profile. "Now," he said. "Tell me what to help."

"Oh. Well . . ." How to say it? She rushed, "You have to help me . . . take Iris." There. A part of it was out. The easy part. The hard part later. In the light of day on a wide sunny beach what she wanted to do with Iris seemed unreal, ridiculous, even to her own hectic blood.

Stashu was completely puzzled. It was such an outlandish thing to ask of him. He couldn't read her face as she was looking out to sea. "Take Iris? For you?" he repeated. "Your papa's Iris?"

"Yes. My father's puppet. I need you to help me steal her. I mean, take her from my father."

He tried to gather his wits, but understood nothing except that this was something important to her.

"Yes, yes, Marta, if you ask I will do. But, please. You can't ask your papa? Say, 'Please. Give me puppet'?"

"No, I can't . . . I want to—" A word came to her. "I want to hide her."

"Ah. Hide. Yes . . . But why?"

"I can't tell you. It's secret. Honest, I can't."

He mulled this over. Then he got it. It was a secret from her father, like the practical jokes his family were always playing on one another. One time his Uncle Petra had pretended he was drunk right before going onstage. Oh, his papa was furious until everybody laughed. Big joke on his father.

"Of course! I understand clear now. We take puppet Iris. Play joke on father, yes? You hide Pinocchio's sister. Hide? For joke, yes?"

Martha stared at him with bottomless relief and admiration. Such a way of putting it had never occurred to her.

Before she could even nod yes, Sparkle Bob had lumbered to his feet and had pulled the leash free of the log. He had evidently decided to catch one of the shorebirds that was feeding at the water's edge. He might have decided to chase them for fun, or perhaps he intended to deliver a few to Lulu as a gift.

"Stop!" Martha cried, jumping up and running after him. She managed to catch hold of the end of the leash as it skimmed along the sand. Half laughing, she was dragged to the cluster of birds pecking in the sand. Sparkle Bob paid her no attention at all. He hardly noticed that there was someone on the other end of his leash.

Mama Pelosi had been dubious about this outing. She had warned Martha: "He weighs more than you do." She had said, "He gets carried away, my Bob does. Even I have trouble, sometimes, holding on to him."

It was Stashu who had reassured her. "Not to worry, Madam Mama, I think will be okay. Lulu takes care. Sparkle Bob is boyfriend. I say to her, 'Get him,' and my Lulu, she get him. No question. Also, I am very strong.''

But Mama didn't tell them that her dog thought he could fly. He seemed to think that if birds did it, he could. He ran after them, and as they lifted, he threw his big weight in the air, snapping and twisting. He didn't seem to doubt he could get up there. The birds swooped around him, circling as if teasing the clumsy creature.

Martha couldn't hold him. The leash was torn from her grasp, and, suddenly freed of the slight tug, he abandoned the idea of flying and sped down the beach on four very swift legs.

As they ran after him, Stashu cried to Lulu, ''Get him!'' and pointed. The little dog raced past them and disappeared in the distance.

Martha was sure Sparkle Bob was gone forever. They would never find him, and it was all her fault. She'd have to drown herself.

Stashu yelled, ''We will find. Don't worry,'' as they raced after the dogs. He was the stronger runner and dashed ahead.

Lulu was the first and easiest one to spot. She was a black dot on the sand. They could also make out the big dog's outline, both animals at rest near a striped umbrella.

''These your dogs?'' asked the lady under the umbrella. Martha had thrown her arms around Sparkle Bob in an ecstasy of relief. She was reprieved. She wouldn't have to drown herself after all.

The white Lab had his head on his paws, next to a baby in a sunbonnet who was digging in the sand with a spoon. The baby was very busy dumping spoonfuls of sand on Sparkle Bob as he lay there. The dog let him. He was entirely unconcerned. In fact, the sand dumping seemed to be some kind of serious understanding between them.

"Nice dogs," said the lady on the beach chair. She flicked her long skirt to better cover her legs. She laughed and said, "I wouldn't mind taking them both home with me. I wouldn't need a baby-sitter."

The day was heating up. The sun was blazing down on the vast lake, breaking into pieces of gold that danced along the ripples, causing the bathers to squint and shield their eyes as they gazed seaward. The beach was filling up with families who would spend the day in and out of the water, or spread out on the sand. There were people now walking along the shore, searching for stranded shells where the receding tide had left a wide ribbon of wet packed sand.

Martha picked up Sparkle Bob's leash. She pulled and yanked but he wouldn't budge away from the child.

Stashu put Lulu down and said some words to her.

The little dog went up to Sparkle Bob and barked a few high yips at him. Then she turned around as if she didn't care one bit what he did. He was on his own.

Whether Lulu told him in some universal dog language, "Get on your feet, you big lummox, you caused enough trouble," or whether the big dog just wasn't going to let the toy poodle out of his sight again, he got to his feet.

The baby's heartbroken cries followed them as they all walked back along the water's edge toward the boardinghouse. Sparkle Bob ambled along with his head down. Now and again he would nudge Lulu with his nose as if to say, "I'm sorry. Hey, sue me. Didn't you ever get crazy and feel like running? I said I'm sorry." Lulu trotted along, nose high, and didn't seem to be forgiving.

As they walked along the shoreline, Martha told Stashu the big problem with this joke on her father. In order to kidnap Iris they needed the key to the carrying case. She explained that Iris was always with him. The problem was, her father was never without the key. He always had it around his neck. "So what do you think, Stashu? How do we get it? What do we do now?"

"Easy!" said Stashu, delighted with himself. His first problem with his new American friend and already he had it solved. "We take case also. Then poof! Who needs key? Iris inside case. Prrresto, no problem." He spread his arms and rolled his *rrrr*'s like a magician.

The boy wasn't prepared for the passionate response this got him. The small girl blazed up at him, crying, *"No!"* so loudly a couple entwined with one another at the water's edge turned to look.

Stashu didn't understand. How could he? He couldn't know that Martha was going to tear Iris apart, bury her deep, close her eyes and mouth forever. She was planning to see Iris dead. He couldn't know that she needed to see that with her own eyes.

"No!" she cried again.

They walked along in silence for a few steps. "Look," she said as calmly as she could. "If we take the case with Iris in it my father would know in a second. He'd see it missing right away. We wouldn't even have time to find a hiding place. Come on, think, Stashu, think of something else. We need to get that key and I don't know how to do it. That's what I came to you for."

The urgency in Martha's voice made Stashu look at her in a puzzled way as she walked at his side, their bare feet splashing in the shallow water. He said to her, "Marta, my English not so good. Also, ways of America I must learn. I want to make clear. This is joke on your papa, yes? He understand is for laugh? Not bad joke?"

59

The open, clear look of goodness on his face made the small girl feel older than he. Older than anyone. She remembered feeling clear and light the way Stashu did. Once upon a time, not so long ago. That was when her father liked her better than Iris, when she was the one on his lap.

She stepped on a shell and it was a relief to be able to groan her pain out loud. There was a heavy nastiness inside of her, a terrible jealousy that she yearned to be rid of. Oh, but she knew what would do it. All she had to do was to get rid of Iris, and she would be her old self again. "Sure, just a joke. The key, Stashu! He even sleeps with it."

"How about take bath?"

"Even then."

This made the boy laugh aloud. "My uncle Petra, he careful man, too. Thief, my uncle Petra. When boy like me, not now. No trust for anybody. He locks for everything. He locks toilet paper too."

Stashu had a wild infectious giggle that made anyone within hearing distance smile. Martha, with an abandon she hadn't known for a long time, threw back her head and gave herself over to a release of tension in a good giggle.

They were still laughing as they stopped at the porch to pull their sneakers back on and entered the house. Mama Pelosi was in the hall, with a bright handkerchief tied around her head as she ran the carpet sweeper over the Persian rug. Sparkle Bob greeted her as if he hadn't seen her in a dog's age. He stood on hind legs and put his paws on her shoulders, licking at her rosy dodging face as if to say, "I'm so happy to see you! It's been so long! The light of my life! Where have you been?"

The woman looked at Martha's flushed laughing face with entire approval. "That's the way, sweetheart. Now you're talking," she said. "All you needed was some of Rosie's good food and a few laughs. For two cents I'd go hunt up your old man and let him see what a smile can do for his kid."

"My father's not old!"

"Oh, sweet pea, that's just a saying. Of course he's not. In fact I think he'd be pretty cute if he ever stopped feeling sorry for himself. Hey, I've been meaning to ask somebody. How was Glenda Blue last night? I never saw her with my own two eyes, but I hear . . ." Rosie glanced around to make sure no one could hear what she said and whispered, "I hear she's a hot number." It was as if they were all the same age.

Stashu looked at her blankly. He didn't know numbers could be hot. He'd have to look that up in his dictionary.

Martha remembered the shimmering creature last night who careened across the stage as she sang her wild song. Her arms were outspread and her head thrown back as she shook and shimmied and sang her siren song. "Follow me if you dare, I don't care, I don't care." Her dress was made entirely of silver beads that looped and swung with her slight body, shooting slivers of light out into the dazzled audience.

Martha would have followed her anywhere. The exciting creature had sent shivers down her back. Then, when Glenda came off the stage, dripping with sweat, she turned into the same frizzy-haired person, plain as could be, who was talking earlier to the stage manager. Magic, Martha had said to herself.

"She was great," Martha told the landlady. "Is my father upstairs?"

"No, he went out. Went down to the five and dime. Said he needed to pick up a few things for Iris."

Martha pulled at Stashu. "C'mon up to my room," she said. "I want to show you something." She took the stairs two at a time. Maybe her father had left Iris behind. Maybe they could bang open the case. Maybe this was their chance.

Rosie called after them, "One of these nights I got to get myself to the theater and see that precious Iris of his."

CHAPTER 7

Of course Iris was gone, case and all. Mr. Rosedale had taken his puppet with him.

Martha sat on her father's bed and leaned her head against the brass bedpost. For a few moments, from the time she had dashed up the stairs and burst into the room, she had the hope that all would be over soon. She would have gotten her hands on her enemy, Iris, done away with her, and the devil inside her would be fed. She would be left in peace.

Stashu came to her and picked up her limp hand. "All right, Marta?"

The beset girl rubbed her forehead. "I'm okay, Stash. I just thought—what we were talking about this morning, you know, about Iris and all. Well, for one crazy minute I thought she'd be here without my father."

"Ah, Marta, you worry too much. I think of way to get her for you. My heart's promise." He laid his hand on his chest. He looked at the alarm clock ticking on the dresser. "I give Lulu lunch and then Pliskas go to theater. Practice time. We take long practice every day. Like this."

From a standing position the boy threw himself into the air, did a double twist up there as if gravity didn't exist for him, and landed neatly on his feet.

This won a slight smile.

Encouraged, Stashu said, "Want to see how Pliskas take walk on street?" He began walking on his hands around the room, doing his best to entertain, watching her face from upside down, looking for another smile.

"You know who you make me think of?" she said. "You'll never guess."

"Who? The President of the United States of America?"

"Yeah, sure. Guess again. Sparkle Bob."

Mr. Rosedale entered the room just then. He greeted the boy, and with a rare show of animation said to Martha, "I bought something special I want to show you."

Her breath caught.

He sat on the bed next to his daughter, fished out the key from around his neck, and opened the puppet case. Martha flashed Stashu a look as if to say, "See? That's the key I'm talking about."

Her father sat Iris on his lap and turned her toward

64

Martha. "What do you see?" he asked his daughter.

"Oh. The ribbons," she said flatly.

The puppet was wearing two new purple bows on either side of her curly head.

"Remember, I was looking all over for this shade? Imagine finding them in this hick town. I knew the color was right for the hair. What do you think, Martha?"

"Yeah, Dad. It looks okay."

Iris turned to Martha. "What do you mean, 'okay'? You can do better than that. 'Hey' is for horses. 'Gorgeous' is the word for me!"

"Now, Iris, I'm sure Martha didn't mean to insult you. Of course you're gorgeous. Tell her, Martha."

Martha shrugged and looked away and said in a small voice, "I don't know."

Mr. Rosedale was annoyed. From the set of his lips he seemed about to say something directly to her. Instead, Iris turned her head this way and that, as if saying to an audience, "Can you believe this?" Then her eyes turned up to his face and she said, "Are you going to let her get away with that? Doesn't she know she's biting the hand that feeds her?"

Stashu saw Martha stare across the room at the mirror over the washstand. What she was looking at was herself and the puppet side-by-side. There was an expression on her pale face that chilled him and he wanted it gone. In a flash he understood that there was something going on between Martha and the painted doll that was no joke.

He took her hand and pulled her up and away from the bed, away from the mirror. He said to Mr. Rosedale, "Excuse please. Martha, we give Lulu lunch, okay?"

"Can I, Daddy?"

Mr. Rosedale was silent for a moment. Then he seemed to regret the exchange they just had. He stretched out his hand, tucked a strand of hair behind his daughter's ear, and said, "Sure. We'll forget about this."

He stopped them at the door. "Hold on. I just remembered. The salesman in the store told me about a little park here at the other end of town that we should see. Maybe one of these days we can take a picnic lunch there before the afternoon show. Rosie Pelosi tells me we should get out more." He laughed shortly and mirthlessly. "Easy for someone else to give advice, yes?" His deep-set eyes rested on his daughter. "How about it? Maybe we'll ask Mrs. Pelosi too." He nodded to the landlady's unseen image as if to say, "There. You can't say I'm neglectful."

Martha's face cleared, and simple joy had her run to twine her arms around her father. "Oh, Daddy, that would be wonderful! We used to have picnics, didn't we? Remember the pedal boat picnic? We kept going around in circles on that big pond. Where was that? People looked at us because we were laughing so much." Another happy thought struck her. "Stashu, you have to come too."

Stashu grinned at the man and his daughter. Hugging he could understand. "I would like. Yes, hot dog!" That was a new piece of slang he had picked up. "But must tell family, yes? You say me when to go picnic, okay? Okay, Marta? I fix."

Rain fell all the next day, Wednesday, crowding the theater but preventing any possibility of a picnic. Thursday dawned as one of those perfect summer days, a dream of a day that made strangers smile at one another on the street. Not too hot, not too cool, fresh breeze, sweet-smelling air, cloudless sky, a bright beautiful world. A picnic day.

The outing was all arranged by the time breakfast was over. Mr. Rosedale had invited the landlady, and Martha had told Stashu. They were all going on a picnic at the town park and would return in time for the afternoon matinee.

By midmorning Martha was in a state of high excitement, anxious that everything and everybody be ready by eleven o'clock, the time they were to set out.

At ten, she was dressed and ready. She knocked on Rosie Pelosi's door downstairs to ask if she could help pack the lunch. Rosie had taken one look at the faded sundress the girl was wearing and drew her into the room. "Tsk, what is your father thinking of, letting you wear such a long, old-fashioned thing. Come in, child, I'm going to take up the hem. Then you can help me choose something to wear."

As Rosie sewed, she sang. Soft words floated on long sweet melodies. Her low strong voice was thrilling to Martha.

While Mama Pelosi sang, Martha was allowed to take out the old costumes that were packed away in a trunk in the corner of the room. They were the ones that Rosie had worn when she was a singer in vaudeville.

Martha had to exclaim over the elaborate clothes. Rosie looked up from her sewing at the excited child. She smiled, crinkling her eyes, showing big teeth. From her came such an aura of warmth and welcome that Martha left the wonderful trunk to move to her, the way you seek the sun when it's cold or step under an umbrella when it's raining.

The dress hemmed, Martha put it back on and gave her reflection in the long mirror a shy approving smile.

Rosie said to her, "Now it's your turn. Help me pick out the perfect thing to wear. You know how long it's been since I've been invited to a picnic? Of course I'm the one that's supplying the eats, but even so. It's an occasion.''

Her bed was a mass of discarded outfits by the time they settled on a powerful print of oversized red poppies. It came to just above her knees, a daring fashion that showed off her ample but shapely legs. A floppy hat framed her strong face. She was all dressed up and shone with pleasure.

''You look beautiful,'' Martha told her, clasping her hands as if in prayer.

''Sure, kid, like an elephant's behind.'' Rosie Pelosi posed herself in front of the full-length mirror again and allowed as how maybe she did look nice. ''Well, not too bad for an old broad,'' she said.

It was time to go. When they stepped out on the porch, Stashu and Mr. Rosedale were already outside and waiting. The boy had practiced with his family first thing that morning so that he could be free.

Rosie Pelosi handed Stashu a large wicker basket to carry. When she noticed that Mr. Rosedale was carrying the ever-present black case with his puppet inside, she threw up her gloved hands. ''Good heavens, do you always have to have that with you? What is it, some kind of growth you can't get rid of?''

Martha was open-mouthed at this. Never had she ever heard anyone tease her father. Even Stashu understood what Rosie had said and laughed. This encouraged Mama Pelosi. She said in mock horror, "Let's get you to the doctor, have it cut off. Or maybe we should buy you one for the other hand so you won't be lopsided. Do us all a favor, Rosedale. Leave the puppet home."

To Martha's astonishment, instead of a show of temper, her father granted the woman a rare offstage smile. He brushed his moustache with a forefinger and said mildly but with genuine puzzlement, "What are you talking about? Iris always comes with me. . . . Somebody could break into the house. Steal her. Then where would I be? I don't have a spare for the act. Don't worry, I won't take her out of her case. Now, come along, and don't make fun. Iris doesn't like it."

From the case came a muffled voice, "I sure don't. Put a muzzle on that woman."

Rosie Pelosi laughed and said, "Shut up, kid" to Iris and took his arm. She wasn't about to start an argument on such a gorgeous day.

Stashu and Martha fell in behind them. He announced proudly, "First time in America, picnic."

"Not peekneek," corrected Martha. "You wouldn't say peek your nose."

"Oh, yes. I say peek nose. Like this, see?" He demonstrated nose "peeking," which happened to be the same no matter what the language or country.

Lulu of course trotted alongside Stashu. Sparkle Bob seemed to be in an agony of indecision. He loped along with his human love a few steps, then pulled on his leash to stay behind with his dog love, Lulu.

"Poor Sparky, look at him, he can't seem to make up his mind. I don't think Lulu likes him."

Stashu grinned at her and she noticed for the first time how shiny and white his teeth were even though there was a funny gap in the front. "My Lulu, she like. If not like, she go . . ." He growled and nipped at the air with bared teeth. "Ho, she bite. Sparkle Bob she not bite. Oh, yes, my little dog, she have big heart for love. Like me." He beat his hand over his heart, saying, "boom, boom, boom."

Martha turned big laughing eyes at him and skipped along in high spirits. Her long braids bounced on her back. Oh, she felt good. Her daddy was in a good mood and Mama Pelosi was so nice and Stashu was her best friend.

When they reached the park, Sparkle Bob was let loose and he and Lulu bounded away. Rosie and Mr. Rosedale strolled along the graveled path. They headed for the cluster of picnic benches on the other side of the statue that stood smack in the middle of the park. It was the hub of all the orderly paths that radiated from it like spokes on a bicycle wheel.

Martha and Stashu stopped and leaned against the spiked iron rail that enclosed the bronze sculpture of a soldier in uniform seated on a rearing horse. It commemorated the local heroes of the First World War.

"Cowboy," Stashu decided. "I love cowboy." In one leap he cleared the dangerous spikes and climbed the statue as easily as a monkey up a tree. He sat himself on the horse in front of the soldier and circled his arm in the air as if in a rodeo. "Yippee!" he cried. "Ride, cowboy!"

"Get down from there!" screeched Martha, torn between laughter and fear of a policeman.

"I take horse home, okay? I train horse for act with Lulu." He was beside her again, grinning like a blond elf.

The picnic, the day, the sun, this funny boy, sent Iris and her own bubbling jealousy right out of her mind and heart. She had almost forgotten what care-free play was like. A giggle burst from her as she tapped Stashu on his arm. "Last touch," she cried, remembering a game of tag.

Before Stashu understood that he was to catch her, she was off and running down the graveled paths to find someplace to hide.

CHAPTER 8

🖤 **S**he ran as fast as she could, a lightness pumping through her, bubbles of laughter rising in her. She could take off like a balloon if she wanted to. One leap in the air and off she would go. But not yet. She didn't want to leave the fine feeling of running. She was the wind and she was headed for the earth's end and would never tire.

"Hey, watch it!" an old man yelled as she dodged around him. She didn't notice that he stood and looked after her. He leaned on his cane and watched the running girl with a grieved smile of memory touching his lips and eyes. Once he too . . .

Three women sauntering down the path on their lunch break broke apart to let Martha dash by. One of them, seeing that the girl was being pursued by a boy still a distance away but gaining, yelled after her, "Faster, kid! He'll get you." Another cried, "Hide!" All three laughed at the game, and, caught up in the playful spirit of the day, joined hands to delay the oncoming boy.

Martha heard them and looked about wildly for a decent hiding place. Ahead she could see the end of her path and the gate that enclosed the park. To one side was a cluster of maple trees and beyond them a tall, fat, flowering bush whose white branches spread out like a hoopskirt from top to bottom. She ran to it at once and, parting the branches, slipped inside the curtain of flowers.

She was suddenly entirely encircled and hidden. It was dim and sweet-smelling under the fall of white blossoms, the sun barely filtering through. The ground was bumpy with roots but there was room enough for her to sit with her back against the trunk of the bush and her legs spread out. A perfect hiding place.

She heard Stashu calling her. "Marta! Marta!" On her knees, she peered out and had to giggle at how funny he looked, searching for her in all the wrong places. She watched him check behind the benches and beat the plantings and stare across the open stretch of grass. He looked back along the path he had come from and then to the gate ahead, shaking his head in disbelief. He even looked up at the sky, as if she might have disappeared into the air.

She recalled a game of Warm and Cold a stage-hand had once taught her. He would hide something, his handkerchief maybe, and she would have to find it by the hints he would give her. If she were getting close to it he would say, "You're getting warm, warmer, you're hot, ouch I'm burning," or the opposite if she weren't. "Uh, oh, you're cold. You'll never find it. You're freezing." Right now she wanted to call out to Stashu, "You're cold. Cold as ice!"

He began to walk back along the path, looking so dejected that Martha relented. She was about to step out of her hiding place and surprise him when he suddenly stopped walking and put his fingers to his mouth. He blew a piercing whistle, once, twice, three times. At that signal his little dog, Lulu, came racing toward him out of nowhere, followed by Sparkle Bob.

Stashu made a gesture and Lulu sat, head tilted at attention, looking up at him with her intelligent eyes. "Marta, Lulu. Find Marta." He let his dog sniff his hand, the one that had held the girl's hand on their walk to the park.

Meanwhile Sparkle Bob was all over the place, licking Stashu's hand, then back to his tiny friend, circling them both. He sat for an instant, his head tilted, copying Lulu. He didn't have a clue as to what was going on.

Smart Lulu seemed to understand what was asked of her. She sniffed and was off, trotting here and there around the path, across the grass, around the trees, her nose to the ground. As Martha watched the search she sent the dog silent hints. Cold, cold, getting warm, warmer, no, cold again.

Meanwhile, Sparkle Bob was sniffing around also. If Lulu wanted to play a game of sniff, then he would too. Martha kept her eyes on smart Lulu. If anyone could find her, she could.

Something poked her shoulder. She jumped in shock and there was Sparkle Bob's big white head thrust inside her flower tent. He licked her face. Oh, yes. He knew this one. What a lucky break, her showing up here.

Stashu was overcome when Martha came crawling out from under the bush. He grabbed her hands, a tremendous grin spread across his face. "Oh, boy. I think gone! Marta whooshh! Nevermore. Good hiding place." He was full of relief and admiration. "Show me," he said.

They parted the branches and stared into the secret space inside.

As she proudly showed Stashu the hiding place she had discovered, she was seized by a tremendous thought. She needed a hiding place for Iris, didn't she? A place where she could bury her for good. Here it was! It was as if she were meant to find it. In her mind's eye a story unfolded as if on a screen. She saw herself running through town all alone at night, carrying Iris, her father asleep in his bed. The puppet's eyes were closed so she couldn't see, and her jaw was shut so she couldn't cry out. Martha saw herself shoving Iris under this bush. And then, with nobody to see her, she would . . .

It came as a relief when Stashu interrupted her wild thoughts. The mind pictures vanished like bubbles as he said, "Let's go to picnic table. I'm hungry like wild animal." Martha looked at him as if awakened. The sun was on her arms and the blossoms on the bush were fragrant. She was hungry, and she had just played a funny trick on Stashu. The dark vision was gone and joy at the fine day once again coursed through her.

Stashu whistled for Lulu and gave Sparkle Bob a thorough body pat and head scratch, saying, "Good dog. Good dog!" Sparkle tried to lick Stashu's nose off. He was ready to accept any praise that came his way, his tail wagging as if to say, "Hey, this is great. What did I do? Tell me so I can do it again."

When they reached the picnic bench Mama Pelosi was busy emptying her basket, putting out bowls of potato salad and coleslaw and a platter of fried chicken.

Near their table was a small playground for little kids, a roundabout, a few swings, and a slide. The roundabout had a number of passengers already, sitting with small legs sticking straight out on the circular wooden seat. A bigger boy with one foot pedaling the ground made it spin around as the children on it shrieked with delight and mock terror.

On a bench in the playground Mr. Rosedale, forgetting his earlier pledge to Mama Pelosi, couldn't resist taking Iris out of her case. The swarming children were a ready-made audience for him to capture. A group gathered around the man with the big doll in his lap.

Out of the doll's mouth came words. She spoke!

"Hi, kids. How are you today? Tennis, anyone?"

With those few words, Iris, the wooden dummy, came alive. The painted smile, the red cheeks, the jaw that moved up and down, the rolling eyes, the wooden limbs, all belonged to the funny fresh little girl on the man's lap. She was real.

A child with his thumb in his mouth took it out to belly-laugh. He wasn't the least surprised that this doll could speak.

One little girl asked, "Can I touch her, mister?"

"Is she alive?"

"Can I hold her, mister?"

"What's her name?"

Iris looked around at the ring of children with her insolent smile. "Okay, okay, keep your hair on, kids. My name is Iris and nobody, but nobody touches me, understand? I only let this guy because he feeds me. Or maybe I feed him.'' She had a high, infectious giggle. Her young audience joined her.

"Now, now, Iris, be nice to these children,'' he scolded, but he also smiled down at her as if he enjoyed her spunk.

He noticed that his daughter, Martha, had turned her back to this performance. She was talking in an animated way to Rosie Pelosi at the picnic table.

He called her over. "Martha, come here, please. I want you to meet some people.''

She reluctantly joined her father on the bench. She sat there, swinging her feet, looking out at the group of children. They stared back at her for a moment without interest. She was just a girl like any other. It was Iris who fascinated them and made them laugh.

Mr. Rosedale sat Martha on his other knee, facing Iris.

"I don't want to, Daddy.'' Martha tried to get down but her father held her.

Mr. Rosedale said to his small audience, "This is my other girl. Martha, say hello to your sister, Iris.''

This was too much. A storm of anger and guilt rose in her, twin furies that she couldn't handle.

"She's not my sister!'' Martha cried, her whole being pushing this insult away. She wriggled once again to get down from her father's lap, but he held her there.

"Sure I am," said Iris directly to her. "Don't we both belong to this guy? Hey, you kids out there, I want you to know he snores like a buzz saw. I hear him right through my carrying case. You tell 'em, Martha."

"Come, come, Iris. I don't want you to teach Martha bad manners. One of you is bad enough. Now, I know my two girls are good friends. Why don't you two sing a song together?" He asked the children, "Would you like that?"

"Yes!" they all chorused, except for a few older show-offs in the back who pretended to vomit.

Martha had never before sat on his knee with Iris. They were face-to-face, the painted smile so close, the blue unblinking eyes looking at her. So knowing, always making fun. Making fun of her.

She stared at that hateful face. Her father, Mama Pelosi, and Stashu, the listening children, the park itself were all forgotten. She spoke straight to the puppet.

"You're not my sister!" she said again, shouting it this time. "If you were, I could beat you up. Yes. I could do . . . do something!" Only Iris filled her eyes and bursting heart. What was bottled up inside her came out as if a cork had been pulled. "Other people have sisters," she cried, "and they can fight, or see who's better, or . . ." She wailed to the open air, "I would have a chance at least!"

She wasn't making sense, and nobody could ever understand. But she couldn't stop. There was no way to say it right and she didn't care. "You!" she said to that grinning, know-it-all face. All the jealousy and hurt in the world was in that word. "I can never catch up. You're it. You're everything. And I can't do anything about it!"

She stopped and stared at her unbeatable rival. Her foot lashed out to kick Iris away. "Get off my father's lap!" She meant that with all her heart.

Mr. Rosedale always kept a tight hand on his puppet's controls. Iris stayed. It was Martha who slid down and ran off, parting the bunch of children, who were laughing, thinking this was all part of the act.

Mama Pelosi stood in Martha's way and caught the girl to her bosom.

CHAPTER 9

🎭 **B**orn and raised in the tradition that the show must go on, Martha was able to get through the matinee that afternoon. She said her words and sang her song and smiled as she was supposed to. She got through it, even though her father hadn't said one word to her since her outburst at the picnic a few hours earlier. When their act was done, Mr. Rosedale went straight to his dressing room without a glance at her, his black brows drawn in an angry straight line.

Martha loitered backstage, still in costume, slipping unnoticed around stagehands who were carrying bits of scenery or performers waiting for their cue. She wandered around the serious working people, stepping over spilling ropes, ducking ladders, and standing props of scenery. Her musty stage dress mingled with the long shadows cast by the naked lightbulbs slung over the rafters.

Out front, just a few feet away, separated from her

by the drop curtain, was the make-believe of the lit stage. She could hear the music of the orchestra and the welling laughter of the audience. In the dim, hushed, workaday world of backstage, the happy noise came to her as if from another planet.

Kazzam the Magician stood in the wings, waiting to go on next. He was in his tuxedo and top hat, checking his props, which were laid out on his collapsible table. He was too busy to notice Martha drifting by him like smoke.

There was no one she wanted to talk to except Stashu. She was waiting for him to finish his act. He had asked her to.

Finally she sat down on the floorboards at the rear of the stage where no one could see her. If there were a rock to hide under she would do so. What filled her thoughts was that her father would never forgive her for the terrible things she had said that afternoon. Iris was his girl and she, Martha, was an outcast. She shivered despite the heat.

In the far corner she saw that the Pliska family was practicing on mats. They were on after Kazzam.

As she watched Stashu work, she thought of what he had said to her on the way home from the picnic. "I know is no joke on your papa to take puppet," he had told her. "I get her for you." Yes. More than ever her enemy was Iris and she needed his help.

After a while she heard the audience applaud Kazzam as he wheeled his table to the wings and ran back onstage again for another bow.

The orchestra struck up once more and she recognized it as introducing the tumbling Pliskas. At that moment she felt a sharp pain in her outstretched foot. Someone had tripped over it.

"Oh, hey, I'm sorry, kiddo. Did I hurt you?" It was Larry Beck, the manager, bending over her, taking her arm, pulling her to her feet. He was a big man with heavy shoulders and a beer belly. Black hairs sprouted from various parts of his body—his ears, his nose, the knuckles of his hands.

Once he decided he hadn't maimed the child, he said, "What are you doing hiding back here? Martha Rosedale, right? Ventriloquist kid?"

He burped as loudly as a drumroll and struck himself on the chest with a fist to aid digestion. "What time is it, anyway?" He tried to read the hands of his wristwatch in the bad light but could not. "Where is that Glenda Blue?" he said to Martha. "I'll tell you where she is. Not here. Take my advice, kiddo. Don't ever be a theater manager. It's ulcer heaven."

The manager patted Martha's shoulder and moved on as he said to her, "Nice talking to you, kid. Enjoyed it. You need something, just ask."

Martha sat again, waiting for the Pliska act to be over. Stashu had told her he was going to talk to his uncle Petra right after the act. He, Stashu, had a great idea for stealing Iris.

She saw the headliner, Glenda Blue, being rushed to the wings by Mr. Beck. She was in her stage makeup. Her frizzy red hair and razzle-dazzle dress made her look electrifying even when standing still.

At last the Pliska act was over. Applause and bravos followed the family as they bounded to the wings and then out to the stage again for the first of many bows.

Finally they were offstage and dispersed to go to their dressing rooms. Martha saw Stashu detain his uncle Petra. She stayed where she was. They were near enough for her to hear what he had to say to his uncle but she couldn't understand a word. The orchestra struck up loud and brassy. Glenda Blue was singing and shaking her way across the stage. It was too noisy. Even if Martha understood the language, she wouldn't have been able to hear what was said now.

She found she didn't need words. Her eyes told her everything. Both Pliskas were so expressive, their gestures and facial expressions so clear, that she was able to understand what was said from their actions.

Stashu, big-eyed, face both apologetic and begging, said what she thought must be, "Uncle Petra, I need a favor."

Uncle Petra clapped him on the shoulder. "For you, my boy, anything. Ask away."

"Remember how you once were a thief?"

Uncle Petra drew back, enraged. His broad, big-nosed face swelled up like a balloon. He roared, "What!" Then quickly looked around to see who could have overheard. No one. The small, watchful girl was overlooked.

Uncle controlled himself and leaned close to his nephew. He said something in a soft tone. "You know that's our secret only. You bring this wickedness of mine to my attention for a reason, of course. Not to shame me?"

Stashu was horrified. "Of course not, Uncle. I need to learn how to break open a lock. I understand you were able to melt a locked vault with your clever fingers. Can you teach me?"

Uncle was all sympathy. "Oh, my poor boy. If it's money you need, count on me." Big hug.

Stashu freed himself, half laughing. "No, no, nothing like that. This is a practical joke we are playing, my friend Martha and me." He stood closer to his uncle and said to his ear, "My friend needs to open a small locked case and we cannot get the key. You needn't ask what's in the case. I promise you it is harmless. A joke on her papa. So I come to you, my uncle. Who else?"

Uncle Petra grinned at his nephew, showing white

slabs of teeth. He nodded proudly. "Who else, indeed? Now, let me see. Harmless, you say? Nothing illegal?"

"I promise."

Uncle stroked his heavy jaw and closed his eyes to think. Then he stretched out his hands, and his fingers arched and curled as if warming up to practice his old craft.

He placed a finger along the side of his nose. He had a thought. "Aha! I have it! Bring the locked case to me. Or better still, bring me to the problem. I, Petra Pliska, ex-thief, now reformed of course, known far and wide in jails all over Europe for my golden fingers, will personally show you the fine art of lock picking. It will be easier to do it myself than to teach you."

"No, no, Uncle." Stashu had his two hands against his uncle's chest as if stopping him from running off that moment. He shook his head vehemently. "This is not for you. What if you were caught fooling around with a case belonging to someone else? People would laugh and the family shamed."

This was quite enough for Uncle Petra. He whispered something in Stashu's ear that Martha couldn't interpret. All she knew was that her friend agreed with a big smile and lots of yeses.

A heavy wave of applause rose from the audience.

The headline act was over. Glenda Blue stumbled off the stage, her face contorted, groaning with pain. She was bent over, unable to straighten up.

The manager ran to her, groaning louder than she was. "Aw, don't tell me! Glenda! What's the matter?"

She screamed at him, "Keep your hands off me, you big gorilla! Get a doctor. I told you those floorboards were loose. That last shimmy did me in. Now my back is out, but good. I'm gonna sue you till your ears drop off."

"Okay, okay, sit down here. Take it easy. Somebody call the doc."

There was general consternation backstage. A circle of performers stood around as the doctor pronounced Glenda unfit for moving a muscle, much less doing her act that night, or any night for the next many weeks. Bed rest and heat. Aspirin and bed. The shake and shimmy girl was out of commission.

When Glenda Blue heard this she got hysterical. "Let me at him," she screeched, meaning the manager. She couldn't tear him limb from limb but she could yell her head off. Meanwhile, as soon as Larry Beck heard she was out of the show, he was gone from her side. He had a major problem to solve.

Stashu and Martha were listening to the performers talk about the disaster. There was sympathy for

Glenda Blue, but everyone seemed to agree that a replacement had to be found in a hurry. The question went from one mouth to another. Who knew of a vaudevillian able to fill in for a couple of days?

It seemed at the same moment Martha and Stashu turned to each other with the same name on their lips.

"You go, Marta," urged Stashu. "Tell Mr. Beck. I can't talk so good."

Martha found the manager pacing up and down in a secluded corner, far from the buzz of the vaudevillians. His meaty hand held his head as if to keep his brains from falling out. The stagehands walked around him, paying him no attention, busy getting the theater ready to close down until the evening performance.

He stopped pacing to speak his worries aloud. "A show to put on and now this! What to do, what to do? Gotta have a flash act. Gotta. I'll have to give money back. I'm ruined. That clumsy dame ruined me. Glenda Blue, my foot. Edna Huggle from the Bronx has ruined me."

He snapped his fingers and brightened as if a light-bulb had gone off over his head. "Call New York. That's what I'll do. See what the Orpheum or Keith can send me. Albee. I'll call Albee." Hope had him wild-eyed.

He noticed that Martha was waiting to talk to him. "Hi, kid. You here to sue me too? I broke your foot or something?"

Suddenly he hit his head with the heel of his hand. "What am I talking?" he said to Martha, as if they were having a conversation. "They can't get a headliner here in time!"

He angled a chair under his big bottom and sat on it, facing backwards. "I need another act. Nine acts with a flash finish. That's what I advertised and that's what they expect. I'm done for." His head sank on his hairy forearms that were folded on the back of the chair.

"Mr. Beck?" said Martha timidly.

"Yeah?"

"My boardinghouse lady. She can sing. She's a wonderful singer. Rosie Pelosi. Ask anybody. She used to, you know, be in vaudeville. She says she knows you."

"So what?" His head sank again. Then lifted. "Yeah, Rosie can sing, all right." What Martha was suggesting seemed to finally hit him. "Maybe . . ." Light dawned and then turned off. "Nah! She's no headliner."

"You ask the Pliskas about that. Stashu told me they have a new finish they're working on. With their dog, Lulu."

This put Larry Beck into deep thought. He pulled

at his lower lip. He said, "I can make an announcement," talking to himself. "I can shuffle. Pliska does the flash, Rosie maybe can . . ." He flung the chair from him and without another glance at Martha strode away, a man with a purpose.

CHAPTER 10

♥ **I**n the dining room of Rosie Pelosi's boarding-house, Larry Beck, the theater manager, leaned his big bottom on the table and held on to Rosie's hand as he tried to convince her to fill in an act for the evening show.

"A return to vaudeville, Rosie. Think of it. Another chance!"

"You're crazy, Larry." Rosie snatched her hand away with a deep embarrassed laugh.

"I mean it, sweetheart. Do it for me."

"Why should I do it for you when I wouldn't do it for my own grandmother?"

"Let me ask you something. At how many rotten parties have I heard you sing? Remember Esther Smugal's wake? You didn't leave a dry eye, my hand to God."

"Yeah. You know why? They were laughing so hard. Larry, I haven't sung professionally in years. I'm scared to death. Get somebody else."

While this was going on, the boarders around the table were quarreling among themselves. As performers in the show, they had a lot to gain and a lot to lose over Rosie filling in for a headliner like Glenda Blue. Kazzam the Magician and Russ Bixler the trick cyclist were against it. The dancing Taylors were for it, as was Mr. Rosedale.

The Pliskas in their native dress were bunched together at the far end of the table like a flock of exotic birds. They were listening closely and not understanding a word. Stashu translated for them and had to raise his voice over the general noise to tell them what was going on.

Martha stayed close to Rosie Pelosi. She leaned against her chair and now and again touched her arm, needing the warmth.

At the sideboard the magician argued with Norm Taylor the dancer. He kept his voice down so the landlady wouldn't hear. "She hasn't set foot on a stage for how many years? She's a grand person and all, but suppose she flops? It's not just Mrs. Pelosi who flops, it's the whole show. Something like that sticks to you like a bad smell. Know what I mean? I'm talking bookings. I tell you it's a chance we're taking."

The dancer replied, "Sure Rosie's a gamble. But I say let's give her that chance. Say we do the show without her. We get an audience who paid good money for a full bill and then we announce we're missing a headliner. They may turn nasty. Want their money back. Beck gives it to them and then where will our money come from? Look, Kazzam, we've all heard her sing. I think she can belt out a song as good as her meatballs and I say she'll bring down the house."

His wife agreed and so did Martha's father.

Meanwhile the theater manager was wooing the landlady, doing his best to convince her. "C'mon, Rosie my love, my little dove, my nightingale. There's no one else within a hundred miles with your experience. Say yes, and tell us what you're going to sing tonight."

Rosie bent down to calm Sparkle Bob, who seemed to have the idea that this stranger was getting a little too close to his idol. He bared his teeth and growled at Larry as if to say, "Back off. Lay another finger on her, buster, and you are dog food!"

"Hush, Sparkle. It's all right. Nobody's going to hurt me. Nobody gets hurt in this house." As she said this she drew Martha to her and looked straight at Mr. Rosedale. She had brooded all afternoon over what had happened at the picnic. Then, from her came the unexpected words: "Sure, I'll sing, Larry."

But Rosie hadn't opened her mouth. She hadn't said a word. At first she was startled, then amused.

Laughing at the ventriloquist's trick, she pointed a finger at Martha's father. "He said it, not me. I'm onto you, Rosedale. Next it will be 'Rosie and Rosedale.' Only you'll be the dummy and I'll do the talking. How's that for a billing?"

"Not bad," said Larry Beck impatiently. He wanted to stick to the point. "Come on, folks, get serious here. What about doing a sing-along? Everybody loves that stuff. 'Sing along with our own Rosie Pelosi.' How about that? Do me this favor. I swear on my mother's grave as soon as I can get a replacement I will. We have only two more days for the run, plus tonight's performance."

"Your mother's grave? Larry, she's not dead!"

"Well, whatever. Do it."

The landlady looked around the table at the performers. They fell silent waiting for her decision. She gave Martha a squeeze and pulled her braid and said in a joking way, "What do you think, honeybunch? You've heard me sing. Will they throw tomatoes at me? Should I go on tonight?"

Before Martha found an answer, the manager told Rosie that the little Rosedale girl was the one who suggested her in the first place.

"What?" Rosie turned to Martha with blazing eyes, not angry so much as surprised. And what she saw in the small anxious face made her forget her own dilemma for the moment. She put a quick hand to Martha's forehead. "What's the matter, child?" she said. "Don't you feel well? Are you feverish?"

"Don't be mad," Martha rushed to say. "I only told Mr. Beck about you because I love the way you sing. I do! So will everybody."

Mama Pelosi wasn't satisfied. There was something about the child that made her uneasy, but the room was waiting for a decision.

Suddenly she was all business. "I need a pianist," she said to the manager.

"You got him. Denby is pretty good. You know him. Chester Denby, the mortician from Elm Street?"

"Can he read music?"

"Does a dog have fleas? No offense, Sparkle Bob."

"I'll get out the sheet music and you see to it that he looks it over. Do we have a chance to rehearse?"

"Whoa. We're not there yet. I gotta get me a flash finish first. Where is that kid? That Stash fella, the foreign kid with the cowlick. He can translate for me."

"Here I am, please, sir, Mr. Beck." Stashu left his family and came forward.

"I'll get back to you," said Mr. Beck to Rosie as he heaved himself away from the table to talk with the

Pliskas. "I won't forget this, sweetheart. I owe you."

"I'll say you do," called Rosie after him. "You owe me about a hundred bucks."

Money was something the performers knew all about. Noreen Taylor said to her, "Don't be a sucker, Rosie. He was paying that Glenda what? Seven, eight hundred at least. Ask for three. What do you think, Norm?"

"What are you talking, three hundred? You got him over a barrel, Rosie. Five hundred at least."

Rosie's blue eyes opened wide at such a monumental sum. Then the realization of what she was letting herself in for came over her. "Costume! I have to see what's left of them." She looked down at her full flesh and made a face. "Anybody have a shoehorn? Help squeeze me into my old gowns?"

She said to Martha, "You want to come with me, sweetie? Help me choose what to wear? You were playing with those old things just this morning."

"Can I, Daddy?"

Mr. Rosedale looked at her coldly. "Do as you please. It's nothing to me." These were the first words he had said to her since her scene at the picnic. They went through to her bones like a cold wind.

Rosie Pelosi glared at him. "We have to have a talk sometime, you and me. Later, when things calm down around here," she said. With another fierce look at the angry man, she took Martha away with her.

Stashu looked up from the conference he and his family were having with Mr. Beck over the flash finish. He said to the manager, "One moment, please."

He left his family, excused himself to Rosie, and drew Martha out of the dining room to the hallway near the stairs. He made sure no one was watching them and in a low voice said, "I have a thing to show."

Out of his pocket he pulled a ring of keys, a mixture of sizes and shapes unlike any other. "Uncle Petra," he whispered. "He give it me. Old thief trick. Keys to open locks. I will find one to unlock Iris for you, yes?"

Martha stared at the keys. She felt nothing, not elation, not relief, not fear, nothing. She nodded dumbly.

"I find time. Your papa, sometime he leave Iris upstairs. I go to room." He took hold of one of the keys and turned his wrist as if opening a door. "I go in, use key, take Iris. I hide for you. Someplace. Okay, Marta? I do this for you?" The boy was taken aback. He thought she would be pleased.

Rosie Pelosi stuck her head in the hallway. "What do you say, Martha? Let's go. I'm nervous as a pup in a thunderstorm."

She and the girl headed for Rosie's private rooms at the rear of the house.

At the front door, just about to leave, Larry Beck said to her, "You're on for tonight. These Pliskas have come up with some finish. Maybe. Let's keep our fingers crossed. See you at the theater by six o'clock, dressed and ready. I have to get hold of Denby at the funeral home. Let's hope he doesn't have a stiff to work on. We have a lot of rehearsing to do."

"My boarders!" cried the landlady. "What will I do about supper?"

"Let 'em starve," said Larry Beck.

CHAPTER 11

There was a long wait between the last few acts at the evening show. The curtain was closed so long that the audience began to show impatience. There was much stamping of feet and whistling. Then the drummer struck a long roll that signaled something unusual was up.

When Larry Beck walked onstage to make an announcement, a groan swept the hall. It wasn't the manager they were waiting to see.

He shielded his eyes against the footlights.

"Ladies and gents, may I have your attention, please."

He had put on a rumpled jacket and tie for the occasion. He looked like a bear in clothes that he had hibernated in over the winter.

There was a restless buzz from the audience as guesses were exchanged about what they were about to hear. It was hot in the theater and the playbills fanned and crackled. Feet shuffled.

"You're in luck tonight!" Larry Beck said, making it sound as if the greatest thing in the world was about to happen. "Miss Glenda Blue was called away on important business. She—" Boos and catcalls drowned him out.

"Yeah—monkey business," This from the balcony.

"What's lucky about it?"

"I want my money back."

Palms down, pushing air, hushing the audience, trying to calm them, he said, "Keep your shirt on. I told you that you were in luck and I mean it. The famous Rose LaRose is with us, the one-time star of many continents, the favorite of monarchs and maharajas the world over. She has consented to sing for us tonight!"

He turned to the wings and gestured to her. "Come on out here, Miss LaRose, and give the folks a treat."

Waiting to go on, Rosie heard this introduction and nearly fainted. "I'm going to kill that man! Now they'll expect something tops. I'll never get out of this alive!"

Martha was with her. She had stayed close to her most of the afternoon, comfortable only in her presence. She said, "Rose LaRose? That's you—I remember."

"Yeah, used to be. Before I married Pelosi. It's me

and I wish it weren't. Why did I ever say I'd do this? How do I look, kid? Never mind, too late now.''

Rosie took a deep breath and swept out on the stage.

At the same time an upright piano appeared from the opposite wing, pushed by two husky stagehands. Chester Denby, the town mortician, followed them, carrying the music. His hair had been flattened to a shine, his tuxedo was pressed, and the only sign of nervousness was the bobbling of his extraordinary Adam's apple, large as a shelf. He spread out the sheet music, put his hands on the keys, and looked up expectantly at the singer.

The audience sat back, waiting to see what they were to be served, ready to boo her off the stage if they weren't pleased.

Rosie leaned against the piano and fanned herself with a large peach-colored feather fan. However nervous she was, it didn't show. She stood quietly, letting them look her over.

What the audience saw was a large confident woman smiling out at them as if who she was and who they were matched perfectly.

The row of lights along the front of the stage lit her like a torch, brightening her eyes, deepening the color of her face and gown, changing her from landlady to vaudevillian.

Martha gazed out at her from the wings as if she

were seeing a stranger. Make-believe time had started.

A high peach bonnet framed Rosie's face. The holes in the peaked hat had been carefully mended and new ribbons sewn on to tie under her chin. No one saw the holes, they saw only a funny old-fashioned hat. Her rose satin dress was from a bygone age, beaded down the front, sweeping the floor, and with a bustle in the back. No one knew that seams had been frantically ripped open and the gown rebuilt from the ground up to make way for extra pounds. What couldn't be mended or hidden was the faded color, the touch of seediness that years in an attic trunk had given it. It didn't matter. She wore it like a queen.

She grinned at the audience and swept her arm down the whole length of her overstuffed body. She said, "Fabulous, huh?"

The audience was won over. They knew she was making fun of herself. When the laughter died, someone recognized her and called out, "Hey, it's Rosie Pelosi!"

"What are you doing up there, Rosie?"

"Rose LaRose, my foot."

Rosie pointed with her fan at the pianist. "Hit it, professor."

At first her voice was unsteady, but it gathered strength. Her hearty speaking voice was, in singing, low and brash, almost a whiskey baritone. It wasn't a pretty voice but it had power behind it. She sang to the rafters,

> *Andy, Andy,*
> *Buy me chocolate candy*
> *And I'll show you what a sweet tooth can do.*

She sang the rollicking "Naughty Angelina, Hit Me with a Tangerina," and "Kick Me Once I'll Kick You Twice." Before long she had the whole theater singing along with her such popular tunes as "Wet My Whistle with a Thistle," "Mister, Sister, Moon," and "That Sweet Old Mother of Mine."

She had no idea how her sunny nature inhabited every song. She had the common touch of a low-rent, lets-have-a-good-time singer, letting the audience know, despite the fancy clothes, that she was one of them.

She was a downright hit.

Martha had slipped from the wings to the back of the theater, where she waited for her cue. The order of the acts had been shuffled around in the emergency, with IRIS AND MR. ROSEDALE in the next-to-last spot. The Pliskas were to do the flash finish.

The solid round of applause for Rosie Pelosi rose all about the small white-faced girl in the old dress. To Martha it seemed to come from far away. She put her two hands together and automatically clapped along with the rest.

Her hands dropped to her lap and she squirmed back in the plush seat to examine them. She spread her fingers. It was as if she had gloves on.

A wave of laughter rolled over the audience, startling her. She looked up. There was her father onstage with his girl on his lap.

When they were in the dressing room earlier, getting ready for the act, the only thing her father had said to her was to apologize to Iris. Martha couldn't remember whether or not she had done it. "I'm waiting for your apology," he had said. "Ungrateful child," he had called her.

Now, onstage, Iris was saying to him, "Why did you take the dictionary away from me yesterday? You always say you want me to learn."

"But you were eating it, you bad girl," her father said, smiling down at her. Anyone could see how much he liked her.

"Well, you took the words right out of my mouth!"

"Isn't she the cutest thing!"

"Smart as a whip she is."

"Pretty as a picture."

Laughter surrounded Martha. A numbness was rising and was her shield.

Iris had just rolled her eyes at the audience and said with that forever smile on her painted face, "Help. Help." The audience knew what was coming and roared along with her: "Help. Help."

Martha didn't mind the laughter and the applause that were showered on Iris. She heard it without the usual burn of jealousy. How pretty Iris was. How clever and smart and funny. No wonder her father loved her best.

Something was rising in her through the numbness, something nameless and terrible. Whatever it was, it was coming.

Martha heard her cue. She gathered her rags about her and ran down the aisle, crying her lines, "Papa, Papa, come home with me!"

She sang, she smiled, she said her lines, she heard Iris sing as if watching herself from the wings.

When the act was over she stumbled off the stage into Rosie Pelosi's arms. The landlady had stayed to see the act. She wiped the cold sweat from Martha's brow.

The Pliskas closed the show. The small change at the very end made a big difference. As usual, they tumbled and spun in the air as the orchestra played their native folk tunes. Then the music stopped. The trumpet blew a fanfare. The human ladder formed with strongman Uncle Petra at the bottom. Papa Pliska jumped from his platform onto the seesaw that catapulted each member of the family onto the shoulders of the one below.

Finally it was Lulu's turn. The big finish was that the tiny poodle trotted from the wings with an American flag in her teeth. She sat on the seesaw and was tossed up and up. Stashu caught her and put her on his shoulders. There, she stood up on her hind legs with the flag in her mouth, moving her head from side to side so that it waved in the air.

The orchestra struck up with "America the Beautiful" and the sentimental and patriotic audience went wild.

Larry Beck was a happy man.

Martha sat at the dining room table of the boardinghouse along with the tired and relieved performers, who were nibbling the night lunch they always had after the show. Even though Rosie Pelosi had been atremble with nerves before the show, she had managed to lay out platters of sandwiches and her famous cherry pie crumble.

"Go to bed, child," Rosie had said to Martha when they returned from the theater.

But Martha pleaded to stay. She wanted the light and noise of the dining room, where the shadows kept to the corners.

Rosie Pelosi had taken off the too-tight gown, but kept on the peach bonnet. Wearing her shapeless apron and elaborate hat, she was both landlady and vaudevillian. She sat at the head of the table with Sparkle Bob's big adoring head in her lap and accepted the congratulations and praise from her roomers with childlike pleasure.

Stashu, who was at the table with the other performers, noticed that Martha's father had returned without the black carrying case. He had left Iris in his room.

When Mr. Rosedale joined the others at the table, Rosie pointed a finger at him and said in a commanding way, "You! I want to talk to you. In the kitchen, if you please."

The talk around the table continued as the landlady and Mr. Rosedale left the room. Stashu whispered to Martha, "I go upstairs now. Get Iris for you. Okay? Our big chance. Your papa busy. I will hide Iris someplace. Where?"

Martha looked at him blankly.

"Okay, no matter. I find good place." Something was the matter with his friend Martha, but the only way he knew to help her was to do this thing for her. He slipped away.

The numbness had wrapped itself around Martha's head like cotton wool. Her heart too. Something soft. It was a relief.

Suddenly, from behind the kitchen door, she heard Rosie yell at her father, "I finally saw your act tonight! How could you? What were you thinking of, dressing that child in rags and spiffing up that wooden puppet of yours! Don't you have any sense? No heart, either? You're so busy feeling sorry for yourself you don't know what's going on under your own nose. Didn't you listen to her this morning? You pay more attention to that stupid puppet than to your own little girl.''

The table had fallen silent. The boarders put their forks down and stared at the tablecloth as if studying it. They didn't look at one another.

Martha heard her father yell back at Rosie. In a strangled voice that was utterly strange to her she heard him say, "Of course I pay attention. What am I supposed to do about it? Iris is my bread and butter. The only thing I'm good for. If Martha has food it's because Iris put it on the table. If she has clothes, Iris put them on her back. You understand that, woman?''

Martha understood it clearly enough. Of course. Iris was the important one.

Sparkle Bob, who hadn't been allowed in the kitchen, had his nose against the door, whimpering.

Then came the worst. Her father shouted in a frenzy, "Don't talk to me about my own child! Martha's a trouper. She knows what the life is. I do the best I can. What else do I have but my work? You tell me. My wife dies. The other one runs off with scum and makes me a laughingstock. Yes, yes—I know how everybody laughs at me. The bitterness is choking me! I'm nothing without the puppet. What else do I have? Without my Iris, nothing. It's the only thing I can do. The only thing I have left!"

And to this Rosie shouted back to him, "There's always love. There's always love."

At that moment Stashu returned to the dining room and bent over his friend to whisper in her ear, "I found good place. On third floor upstairs. Room for old things. Was locked but Uncle Petra key open. I leave open for you. Iris is on rocking chair."

The shadows were thicker now, moving away from the corners. Martha slid away from them and ran upstairs. Iris was waiting for her.

CHAPTER 12

Martha glanced about the well-lit landing on the second floor of the boardinghouse for a way to go even higher. Stashu said he had hidden Iris on the third floor. She had never been up there.

Opposite the row of guest rooms in the hallway, she saw a narrow flight of uncarpeted steps at the far end. She climbed up and at the top was a door. She opened it to a smell of darkness and dust, and to a chilled gust of air despite the evening's heat. Her hand brushed the wall to the side of the door and found the light switch.

She was in a room at the top of the house. It had cracked plaster walls and bare rafters, and a few trunks and suitcases piled in a corner. Boxes of Christmas ornaments sat on a discarded dresser. Winter clothes hung from a pipe across a wall.

On a rocker with one missing rung sat Iris.

Martha sighed and stared at the puppet. Here was her enemy. She remembered how it hurt to look at her. That was why she was going to take Iris away, hide her, do away with her, step on her face so she wouldn't be so pretty. Step on her mouth so she wouldn't be so smart and funny. Get rid of her so that she, Martha, would have a chance.

She shivered in the chilled air. Was it Iris or her own voice that she heard say, "Oh no, you don't want to do away with me." Iris's eyes were open, staring straight at her.

"I don't?"

"You don't want to kill me, silly girl. You want to *be* me."

Be Iris! Oh yes, of course. How dumb Martha was not to know right away that was what she wanted. If she were Iris she would be the one to sit on her father's lap. He would straighten her dress, fix her hair, and pay attention to her. She would have applause and laughter from everyone. She wouldn't have this terrible want, this burning inside her. Her father would love her again.

"But look at me. I'm not pretty. I'm not smart. I don't have yellow curls. He'll know."

"Then take mine."

Martha didn't know if Iris held it out to her of if she tore it away herself.

The blond wig was in her hand. Now it was Martha who had to hide. She flew down one flight of steps and then the others. People were still talking in the dining room. No one saw her open the front door and leave the house.

She ran through the half-deserted streets. Street lamps flickered above her, dimly lighting her way. There were a few strolling couples, but it was after ten o'clock at night and most of the holiday families were in bed. Occasionally she passed windows that were lit behind drawn shades. Once in a while a car passed by, sometimes filled with shrieking teenagers out joyriding. Mostly it was quiet. No one noticed her. There was no earth beneath her feet, no sky above her head.

The insistent smell of seaweed that drifted around the town was a constant reminder of the vast lake nearby. The metallic odor was carried by a breeze that gave Martha a gentle push to where she was headed.

She knew where she had to go. Didn't she find the perfect hiding place in the park with Stashu? It had white flowers cascading down like a waterfall. The flowers hid everything. She'd be safe there.

As Martha ran toward the park, she had to stop now and again to check her balance. Her legs were getting stiff. She slowed to a walk. By the time she reached the flowering bush, she was tottering. Her neck ached too. It was too hard to turn her head, so she stopped doing that. She parted the curtain of flowers with difficulty because her arms didn't work. Down she dropped to the bare earth.

She leaned her head against the thick stem. It was bumpy but she didn't feel it. She sat and waited for whatever happened next.

Stashu waited in the dining room for Martha's return. The group around the table was still there, listening in on what was going on in the kitchen. Rosie and Mr. Rosedale were still at it.

The boy thought Martha probably went to bed. He went upstairs and knocked on her door, the door he had so recently opened to steal Iris. No one answered and he wasn't about to pick the lock again.

He began to be uneasy.

He checked the storage room on the third floor that he had unlocked for Martha. A quick glance showed him the puppet was still there. Something was different about her. The next instant he realized she was without her blond curls. Martha must have been up there.

But then, where was she? He had practically banged on the door of her room. She surely would have heard him if she were there. Where else could she be? Worry clutched at him. A taste of fear in his throat.

He returned downstairs to the dining room. At

that moment Mr. Rosedale emerged from the kitchen. He was paler than usual, his eyes more fierce. He glanced around at the assembled group of boarders. They were doing their best not to look at him, and he understood at once that his terrible exchange with the landlady had been overheard. With a stiff goodnight nod he was about to leave the dining room when Stashu stopped him. The boy told him that he couldn't find Martha.

"She's in bed," Mr. Rosedale said gruffly.

"I . . . how you say . . ." Stashu showed how he knocked on the door. "So much noise. She wake up!"

"Well, she's a sound sleeper. I'm going up myself. Good night all."

In a matter of minutes he had returned. "She's not there! My girl isn't in our room. Anybody see her, know where she is?"

Rosie came out of the kitchen, hearing this. Her eyes were bloodshot and there were two hectic spots of red on her cheeks, a leftover from the fight. Now alarm was added to her upset. "I knew it, I knew it," she cried.

They called out Martha's name, and the boarders made sure she wasn't in any room of theirs. If she weren't in the house then perhaps she had gone outdoors.

An idea occurred to Stashu. "I tell my Lulu to find

Marta, she find. I know is poodle, not hunting dog, but she very smart. Okay?''

The dog was given one of Martha's socks to sniff. Sparkle Bob sniffed at the sock, too.

Stashu gave Lulu the order to find Martha. The little dog put her nose to work and went right to the chair that Martha had sat on. Then she went to the front door.

There she stopped and seemed to be puzzled. Several times she went from the door to the foot of the stairs and then back again. Finally she seemed to have decided. She left the door and scrabbled up the stairs to the second floor of the boardinghouse, with Sparkle Bob bounding along after her.

''That dog is headed for my room, and I tell you she's not there,'' said Mr. Rosedale.

Lulu didn't stop at the room. She raced along the landing to where the flight of narrow steps led to the storage room. The scent she was after got stronger and stronger. Up the stairs she leaped, her nails clicking on the wood. The thick door didn't stop her. It was partly open, and she nosed her way in with Sparkle Bob right behind her.

Rosie Pelosi paused on the second-floor landing when she saw the dogs head up to her storage room. ''Well, that's another dead end,'' she said to the gathered boarders. ''That little girl can't be in there. The door is always locked.''

A shattering cry from Mr. Rosedale had them freeze in place. The ventriloquist had seen what Lulu had in her teeth.

The small dog dropped the puppet at Stashu's feet. Lulu had never made such a mistake before. The boy couldn't understand such a mixup. Martha and Iris. His smart dog had mistaken one for the other.

Stashu confessed that he had taken the puppet and had hidden her in the storage room. Rosie Pelosi firmly stopped any further explanation. That would have to wait. She said that for now the only important thing was to find the child. Mr. Rosedale nodded his agreement. He hurried to return Iris to her case and was back right away.

Stashu had Lulu in his arms, stroking the curly black fur, thinking of where his desperate friend might be. All he wanted was to find her and make her feel better, make her smile. Like dumb, eager Sparkle Bob, Martha had said. When was that? On the picnic.

Stashu realized where to look for Martha.

He told Rosie and Mr. Rosedale about the hiding place in the park. "Marta, she love secret place. She hide good. I know where she go. Come, I show you. Quick, quick."

Rosie Pelosi gathered a few flashlights from the

kitchen. The landlady, Martha's father, and the boy set out.

They hurried through the dimly lit streets to the blackness of the park. Once there, only their flashlights guided their steps.

Stashu knew exactly where to go. They ran down the path toward the flowered bush, Martha's hiding place. Rosie Pelosi had to stop to catch her breath and clutch at her heart. A terrible foreboding gripped her.

The boy found the bush, and all three plunged under the cascade of sharp-smelling flowers. Their flashlights played on the girl.

She was stiff-legged on the ground, a smile fixed on her heartbreaking face. A sorry bunch of golden curls sat on her head.

She looked up at her father, and at Rosie and Stashu as if at an audience. She rolled her eyes at them as if to say, "Am I not pretty and funny and all anybody could want to be?" Then she rolled her eyes at her father and dropped her jaw up and down to say what she was known for. She said what always made people laugh.

"Help, help," cried Martha. "Help, help."

EPILOGUE

♥ **F**ee, Faw, Fum, the story is done.

It is ten years later. We are now in a ghost theater. Vaudeville is long gone. It has been pushed off the stage by the popularity of movies.

The audience of shadows shouts approval as the houselights dim. The orchestra strikes up. The curtain rises once again.

A placard announces, IRIS AND MR. ROSEDALE.

Mr. Rosedale walks out on the stage. A single spotlight follows him. He holds Iris carelessly by an arm, dangling her at his side. His tuxedo is shiny with age. His moustache droops. Iris's dress is dirty.

He walks to a chair in the middle of the stage and sits. He looks out at the audience and says to his puppet, "Say hello, Iris."

"Hello Iris," repeats the puppet.

She laughs and rolls her eyes at us and her mouth opens to say her famous line, "Help, help." Nothing comes out. The ventriloquist struggles, but can't bring himself to say the dreadful words.

Iris looks up at him and says, "You lost her, not me."

"You, me, what's the difference?" says Mr. Rosedale. He rises and takes a step to the wings. He says to his puppet, "We're a great pair. Too bad we died some years ago."

From the audience a heckler yells, "You said it! Onstage and off."

Laughter rolls around the theater, and at this familiar sound, Mr. Rosedale's head lifts and a faint smile crosses his melancholy face.

"Hear that, Iris? What a great sound laughter is. They want you to sing."

Iris sings from his arms as he walks toward the wings. The spotlight follows, but now it doesn't seem quite as bright. At first his beautiful voice is unchanged. With each step it falters and cracks. By the time he leaves the stage, he is wheezing the song.

A piano is pushed onto the stage. The placards at the side announce, ROSE LAROSE.

Her flesh is softer now, and she is slower of movement. But her smile could still warm a stone and she lights up the stage with her good humor. She waves her feather fan at the pianist and says, "Hit it, professor."

With the first notes a bark is heard from the wings

and Sparkle Bob limps out on the stage. He nuzzles her hand, delirious with joy at being allowed to join her.

Again the piano begins and Rose LaRose sings,

> *I took her in*
> *I made her mine*
> *And now she's grown*
> *And now she's fine.*

The last line of her song is somewhat muffled. The stage is darkening. Rosie says to the audience, "We don't have much time. We must hurry."

She waves a hand at the gauzy drop curtain behind her. It rises. We see a replica of the front porch of her boardinghouse.

A young man approaches the porch. His face is bony, sharp-nosed, eager. But his feet drag. He's nervous. He has the wiry body of a trained athlete. His hair is the color of straw. He mounts the porch and knocks on the door.

It is opened by a young woman with long dark hair and a steady gaze. She is more striking than pretty. Her eyes have both depth and liveliness. They take in the young man before her.

"Martha?" he says. Then he corrects himself. "No—Marta."

She smiles. "You speak better than I remember."

"And you look better than I remember."

We can barely hear them, barely see them. The footlights are dimming fast. We see them sit together on the porch steps and begin to talk as the curtain slowly falls for the last time.

The show is over. It is time to leave. Vaudeville is dead, but not hope. And never love.

J
Slepian,
Pinocch

J
Slepian, Jan
Pinocchio's sister

B AUG 25
APR 10

J48921   6949